Tales from Jevlir:
Oddballs

Henry Neufeld

Enzar Empire Press
P. O. Box 841
Gonzalez, FL 32560

enzarempire.com
pubs@energion.com
(850) 525-3916

ISBN10: 1-893729-26-5
ISBN13: 978-1-893729-26-1

Library of Congress Control Number: 2009936876

Cover Design: Jason Neufeld (jasonneufelddesign.com)

Enzar Empire Press
P. O. Box 841
Gonzalez, FL 32560

Web: enzarempire.com

pubs@energion.com

Enzar Empire Press is an imprint of *Energion Publications*

TABLE OF CONTENTS

PREFACE

I wrote these stories for fun. I collected them into this booklet for fun. Since I own a publishing company, I had the means at hand to produce it easily.

Most of the stories come from my fiction blog, The Jevlir Caravansary (www.jevlir.com), though they have been edited and revised for inclusion in this volume. I wrote two stories, *A State of Mind* and *Seeker of Justice* specifically for this book.

The stories may seem a little bit unusual. What I have tried to do in each story is to introduce some aspect of the culture of the Energion world, or to some particular character I found interesting. Because of this I have added a glossary (yes, in a collection of short stories!) because some elements of the background may not be obvious to the reader, and their explanation within the text may be cumbersome.

I also tried to make all events and actions fit within the rules of the original Energion Role Playing Game. You can find the manuals for this game at http://energion.hneufeld.com.

The world in which these stories are set is a fantasy world of magic, gods, swords, and sorcery. The gods are often quite prominent. You may wonder whether these stories generally have Christian themes and whether they are allegorical. If you find any allegory in these stories at all, it is of your creation, not mine. I intend nothing allegorical.

Some religions in this fantasy universe will resemble some real-world religions. Some cultures will resemble real-world cultures, particularly those of the ancient near east. This similarity is not accidental, but in all cases, without any exception, I have modified substantial aspects of the religion and culture in question. For example, in the ancient near east many sun religions have a focus on justice. The Ecumenical Temples of the Sun occurs in a couple of these stories, and is an organization of such religions, but will not match any single ancient near eastern religion.

Similarly, friends who know I read Hebrew tend to find Hebrew references. There are some uses of Hebrew and ideas from Hebrew scripture, but none of the words in this collection that might appear to have a connection to Hebrew, such as the city of Shalem or various words ending in -im actually do.

One other point that might confuse is my use of measures. I use a variety of units, including both metric and U. S. measures of distance. This reflects the variety of measures that are used in the places where these stories are set, and helps demonstrate some of the confusion. Check the glossary for any measures or monetary units that do not have real-world equivalents.

Do I intend morals in these stories? Not in the sense of each story having an intended lesson. What I do require of myself is that I create a world in which actions have consequences and that moral decision making is important. That moral decision making is done in a very different culture, with different customs and different laws. This doesn't mean that my bad guys never get away with anything, but you'll know that they did!

I hope you enjoy yourself reading these stories, and that you don't take them, or me, too seriously.

– Henry Neufeld, Gonzalez, FL August 10, 2009

DEDICATION

To all the players in the original role-playing game who put up with my endless tinkering with the politics and background, not to mention weekly handouts containing rule revisions.

It was fun—for me at least!

Glossary

Aagerinar – a duchy of the now defunct Malkuthim Empire which still calls itself a duchy even though it is completely independent. It's capital is the East Enzar port city of the same name.

Ardenean – can refer to a citizen of the Ardenean Empire but more commonly refers to a cultural practice or a person that comes from that continent.

Ardenean Empire – once occupied most of the continent that shares its name and now occupies the north central area. There are dozens of former provinces that now form independent nations around it.

Ardenus – a large continent in the northern hemisphere that is best known for the once large Ardenean Empire and the large number of cultures derived from it.

Avim – a race of Enzaru extraction generally most commonly involved in intellectual activities, but when found in dominantly human areas often involved in crime.

Caravansary – a place where caravans can stop, rest, and resupply.

Challenge – a legal maneuver similar to an objection in Enzar derived legal systems, except that the record is not corrected, though a challenge can stop further testimony along the same lines.

Ecumenical Temples of the Sun – an east Enzar religious group that combines sun worship from several cultures. It is a proselytizing religion.

Enzar – (1) a continent largely in the northern hemisphere. It consists of three major areas, the main continent, East Enzar to the northeast and south Enzar to the southeast. (2) the name of a culture that originated on that continent. (3) an empire that once ruled almost the entire area. (4) a language family that descends from the ancient Enzar language.

Enzaru – A person of the Enzar race. The same form represents singular and plural, an Enzaru, many Enzaru, the Enzaru.

Eselena – a province of the Ardenean Empire until it declared independence following the Kachadahz war.

Galiru – known as water people, a species of humanoid that prefers living near lakes and streams. There is a substanial population of Galiru south of Aagerinar.

Half-Kal/Half Kahl – a cross between a Kal and a human. Since most species interbreeding occurs between humans and one of the less numerous groups, "half" with only one species name specified always referred to half human and half some other species.

Impies – a derogatory nickname in provinces and former provinces for Ardenean Imperial troops who are not known for their competence or reliability.

Jevlir – a town on the caravan route from Aagerinar leading westward across the Enzar continent. It is the last secure supply stop for westbound caravans. It is technically subject to the Duke in Aagerinar, but not everyone remembers this.

Kachadahz – A nation primarily populated by giants but with some recent human alliances

Kal/Kahl – a humanoid species known generally for their violent nature.

Kallasia – island kingdom off northwest Ardenus.

Kelaru – a woodland people of Enzaru extraction.

Malethia – city and territory immediately to the south of Aagerinar.

Note – a legal maneuver in Enzar derived legal systems that allows an advocate to place objections and counter-evidence into the record immediately rather than waiting for cross-examination or for his own case.

Shalem – port city on the western Ardenean coast, nearly directly across the ocean from Aagerinar on the eastern Enzar coast. Known as a haven for criminal gangs, pirates, and merchants with a less than savory reputation.

Sidroc – a town at the north end of the Ford Island which is just off the coast east of Aagerinar. The bay between the island and the mainland forms Aagerinar harbor.

Sovereign – a coin of the new defunct Malkuthim Empire, of which Aagerinar was once a part. A sovereign is made of silver and weighs about an ounce.

Valor – the standard monetary unit of Aagerinar, issued by the Ducal mint. It is about 1.5 ounces of silver.

Tlazil – an amphibious intelligent species that is a bit larger than standard humans.

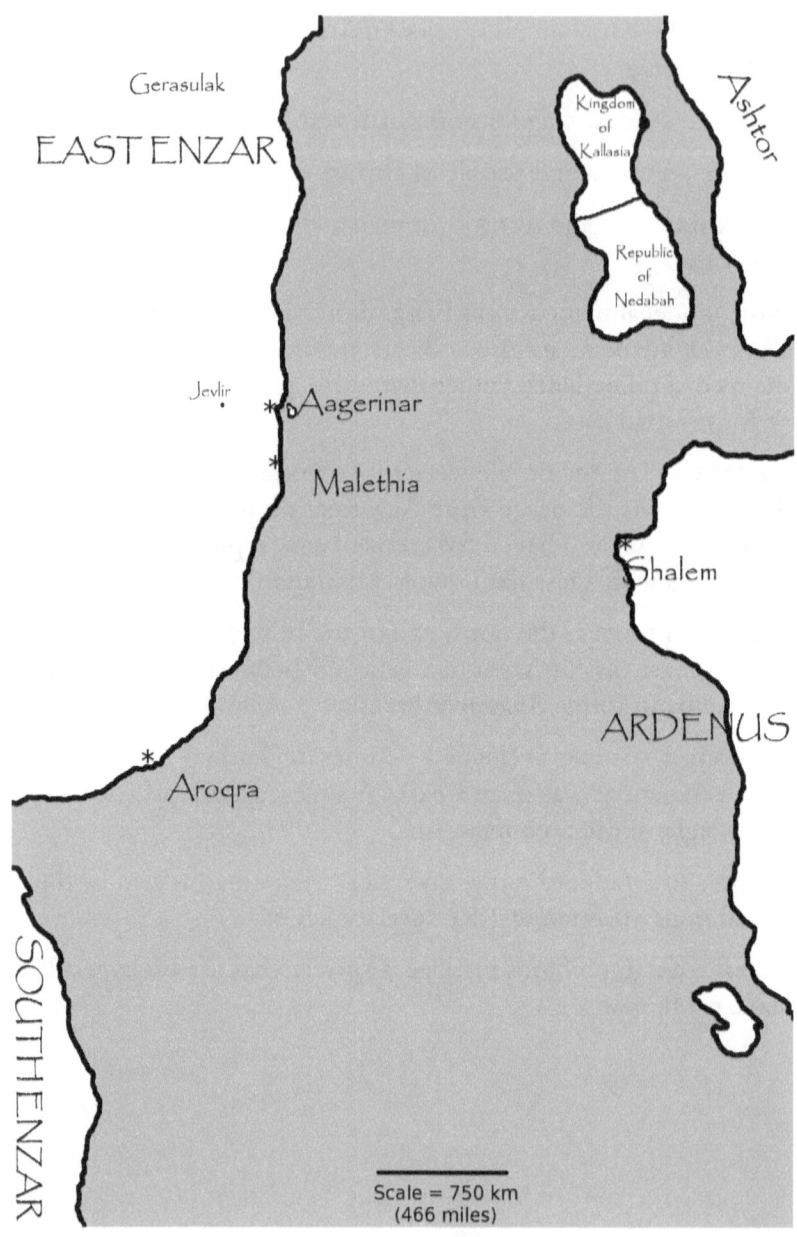

SIMPLE RISK

A miss is as good as a mile, but much more nerve wracking!

Jerin, legal advocate, could not quite believe the young woman facing him across the table. They were in the Aagerinar city jail, and he had been asked to take her on as a client.

"Marita, heir to the Earl Northmarch, and also third in line for the Duchy of Aagerinar," he said, reciting the known data. "How old are you, anyhow?"

"Rumor has it I'm 15." Her expression didn't change. She was relaxed, even serene. There was no sign of the tension he would expect of a young woman under arrest.

"Rumor has it? Don't you know?"

"My adoptive mother guessed I was eight when she adopted me. That was seven years ago. In actuality, nobody knows for sure." Very slight amusement showed. He suspected that if this girl did know, she wouldn't be telling. "But none of that is important right now. I need you to do some work for me." She did not say "represent me" or "defend me."

"If I'm to represent you," he said, "You'll need to follow my instructions exactly and trust yourself completely to my care. You are charged with a serious crime, and it's under the city jurisdiction, not the ducal, so it won't be easy."

"On the contrary," said Marita, "You'll do exactly as *I* say, speak when I tell you to, and be quiet when I want you to. You will merely be a voice." It was amazing how, when you started from the original serenity, slight changes could convey a great deal of meaning. Now there was a hardness in her expression that would permit no argument.

"Someone your age can't do that!" he said. "The legal system can be complicated, and you can't count on your family name to save you from this one. City judges aren't chosen by the Duke and aren't susceptible to the kind of influence you're used to using."

"I can get someone else. Or you can sit beside me, win this case, and get the fame that results. It's your choice. But remember, I don't deal well with disloyalty. You'll agree to do things exactly as I say." Still that hardness around the lips.

Jerin considered for a few moments. He could end up looking like a fool, but on the other hand, Marita had the reputation for living a charmed life. She was close friends with the Ducal heir, her mother was the High Priestess and founder of the Ecumencial Temples of the Sun, and her father was the Earl Northmarch. The odds she was going to end up swinging by the neck from the end of a rope were probably small.

"OK," he said. "I'll do it. But please let me give you some advice along the way."

"You can always give me advice, provided it's not at an inconvenient time." The serene smile was back again. "But it won't make any difference. You see, I already know how it's going to go."

There was a moment of silence, and then she continued. "I'll be arraigned today, and you'll ask for bail. You don't need detailed instructions for this. My mother will be present and will be willing to present the bail in cash. I'll be released and take up residence at the Aagerinar *Ecumenical Temple*. We will then demand a jury trial ..."

"Oh no! my lady," Jerin interrupted. "Not a jury trial. You don't understand. Jury trials are messy. The jury is selected randomly in the presence of the court. They draw 21 names at random, then each side gets to dismiss jurors alternately until there are seven. A simple majority of four is required to convict. It can't be controlled."

"We'll demand a jury trial," continued Marita, as though the interruption had never happened. "After that you will have nothing to do until you appear with me on the defense. I will, of course, be associated in my own defense, and you will be there to advise me. I will chat with you frequently, thus demonstrating how important your expert advice is to me."

"But a jury trial, my lady! The rules of evidence go out the window because the jury can override the judge's decision. That's why jury trials are so rare."

"Nonetheless, it's a jury trial that we will have." No give, no reaction to what he was saying. He reconsidered his decision to be associated with this mess, but again he remembered how many times this girl had landed on her feet in tough situations. It was unlikely she had suddenly become totally insane. Surely she had some control over the jury selection process. That had to be it. Impossible as it might seem, the jury *would* be rigged.

It was the day of the trial. Aagerinar city trials were required by law to be accomplished in a single session. One rule the jury was not allowed to override was that the defense got the same amount of time as had been allowed to the prosecution. This tended to make the jury a little bit careful as to how much time they allowed the prosecution to present its case. It also tended to make defense teams very wary of taking too much of their legally permitted time, lest they annoy a tired jury. Legal advocates diligently avoided jury trials under the city rules; a trial by a panel of three judges was the alternative, and resulted in generally fairer trials.

Marita signaled quietly to Jerin as to which seven jurors to exclude. As she did that, he became even more convinced that she must have the process under control. There was no apparent logic to who she was excluding from the pool. Since no questions were permitted during the exclusion process, most advocates simply used this option to guarantee randomness in the jury selection. Marita seemed to think she was making informed selections.

With the jury seated, the prosecution began their case. The lady Marita had been arrested on a street two blocks from the Serenta Bank, wearing ragged street clothes and dirty as a street urchin. She had been carrying three gold bars, which would be introduced into evidence and identified as having come from the aforementioned Serenta Bank. She had refused to identify herself. By the time the police had discovered her identity, they had also found that the Serenta Bank had been robbed, that significant records had been destroyed, and that several safety deposit boxes were missing. He would establish a motive of greed, based simply on the lady's reputation. He would establish opportunity based on her location, means based on her abilities, and culpability based on her possession of some of the stolen money.

Jerin was sure he saw a smile playing around the edges of Marita's face as the prosecutor gave this account. The chief city prosecutor was making the presentation, and Jerin admired the careful lines of his case as he spoke. It was a masterpiece of legal presentation. The terminology was entirely correct and unambiguous. It was regrettable for someone like Marita that testimony of reputation was permitted in Aagerinar courts. Her reputation for getting out of jams would hurt her, and the prosecutor could play on it. He wasn't looking at the jury–they looked bored, and they didn't understand much of the terminology.

Marita insisted on presenting her own opening. It was short. "Fellow citizens of the jury," she said, "In my defense I will show that the prosecutor is not only stuck up and boring, he's wrong about nearly everything."

Prosecutor: "Challenge!"

Judge: "On what grounds?"

Prosecutor: "That is an improper and insulting opening statement."

The judge was more aware of his surroundings, and could see the interest of the jurors. But he also knew that while there were a number of arguments that could be made against an opening statement, the only one that was usually successful was an argument of irrelevance, that the advocate was talking about completely irrelevant issues. In this case, though eccentric, the opening would probably be allowable by a panel of judges. Furthermore, an objection after the fact in front of an Aagerinar city jury was usually a waste of time–the words were said, and an alteration of the record was not permitted. He could tell Marita to stop, and probably be overridden by the jury, but she had already sat down.

"I'll note your challenge," he said, "But that's all that can be done at this point.

Marita's eyes were on the jury, communicating with them in that subtle way she had with her facial expressions.

The prosecutor became more and more surprised as Marita failed to challenge his basic testimony. There was a witness from the Ducal army who testified to Marita's work instructing commandos in urban warfare and evasion, along with her intimate knowledge of locks and traps. The prosecutor expected her questioning to try to obscure her skills, but instead she used the time to emphasize the breadth and depth of her knowledge and experience. She got him to say that he regarded her as the foremost authority in the Duchy on building security. In the end, she asked him how likely he thought it was that she would be arrested within two blocks of a crime she actually committed. "Never!" he answered.

Then there was the lead officer of the guard patrol that arrested her. The prosecutor couldn't think of anything Marita could gain questioning him. There was no doubt about who she was. But Marita did have one question:

Marita: "Which way was I walking when I was spotted by your guards?"

Guard: "North."

Marita: "*Toward* the bank?" (Pause)

"Yes."

There was the bank officer to identify the gold bars. They were stamped with the Serenta Bank's logo and numbers. They were the type of bars that would be in the bank. He could not verify that they were actually bars that were in the bank at the time because the vault records had been destroyed in the robbery, but he was as certain as possible that they were.

Marita: "How much money was stolen from the bank?"

Manager: "Fifty bars of gold, and an unknown amount from the safety deposit boxes."

Marita: "Where do you suppose I hid the other 47 bars?"

Manager: "I have no idea. I'm not a thief!"

Marita: "I was just curious. I'd really like to go back and recover them, but I have no idea where they are!" (laughter)

Marita: "I'm showing you a document, and I ask you to identify it." (hands witness a sheet of paper with an embossed seal on it)

Manager: "It appears to be a receipt from our competitor, Bank of Aagerinar, for the withdrawal of 10 gold bars. It's dated three days prior to the robbery."

Marita: "Can you read the numbers on that sheet and compare them to the numbers on the three bars of gold I was carrying when arrested?"

Manager: "Yes I can. (long pause) The three bars are listed here."

Prosecutor: "May I point out to the court that this receipt has not been verified by anyone and has, in fact, been in the possession of the defendant?"

Judge: "You may, and the jury may consider that fact."

Jerin was reasonably certain that despite the questions, most Aagerinar juries would convict based on the evidence available. The receipt was too convenient, and the prosecutor's suggestion that it might be forged was reasonable. In fact, it looked very much to him like evidence Marita had planned the job carefully. But he knew that the next stage, personal reputation, would be very telling. He and many other advocates wished that evidence of reputation was not allowed in Aagerinar city courts. It was not according to precedent even the loose "precedent from anywhere" method used throughout the Duchy. But the city had passed a specific ordinance allowing it because so many criminals were known to have committed a variety of crimes, but there was insufficient evidence to convict them of specific crimes. Nonetheless, it also permitted the innocent to be convicted without evidence as well.

On the other hand, as much as he wanted to win this case, he himself was now convinced Marita had committed the crime, and even planned this entire scene. He knew she'd done it, and he was convinced now she was going to be acquitted.

The witness the prosecutor called as to reputation was an advisor to the city prosecutor's office. This was unusual, though legally permissible. The jury could ignore such testimony because of the witness's bias, but they rarely did.

After testifying to the number of crimes in which Marita had been suspected, or rumored to be involved, the prosecutor moved to a new line of questioning:

Prosecutor: "Hasn't Marita's own father cut off communication?"

Marita: "Note!"

The "note" was a legal maneuver traditional in Enzar courts and allowed in Aagerinar courts that allowed opposing counsel to make it clear that they intended to challenge a point of testimony and how they intended to do so, without allowing time for the point to settle in jurors' minds. Jerin had been unaware that Marita was acquainted with it.

Judge: "Your note?"

Marita: "May I ask the prosecutor why he is eliciting testimony about my father's attitude from this witness when my father himself is available?"

Jerin saw red flags in front of his eyes. Danger! Danger! The prosecutor would probably like nothing better than to get Lord Kaltros on the stand to comment on his attitude toward his daughter, an attitude that was well known. Having her father call her a thief in person would guarantee a conviction! But it was too late.

Prosecutor: "I felt it unnecessary to call Lord Kaltros when his attitude is a matter of public record."

Marita: "Let me inform the, um, honorable prosecutor that should he persist in this course of action, I will call my father so we can hear his testimony for ourselves."

The prosecutor's expression went through annoyance, to concern, to fear, and then back to blank.

Prosecutor: "I do not wish to disturb the Lord Kaltros. I will abandon this line of questioning."

The closing statements were predictable. The prosecutor presented a logical masterpiece, spinning every single event in his own favor. Marita simply pointed out that the prosecutor had placed her no closer than two blocks from the crime scene, had claimed that she was in possession of materials stolen from the bank, which turned out to be legally hers, and that they had tried to impugn her reputation, but she was proud of her service to the duchy. She noted that the city guard didn't really like the ducal forces and was also known to be more determined to make *any* arrest than it was to make the right one. As she said it, she made eye contact with each of the jurors in turn. She fairly caressed them with her eyes and the expressions on her face.

The vote came in four to three for acquittal.

After Jerin received the congratulations of his peers for a masterful strategy, though an eccentric one, he met with Marita.

"How did you do it?" he asked. "It is pretty much a given that one can't rig a jury under our system. Did the court clerk owe you a favor or something?"

"Indeed she did," said Marita.

"But how could she arrange it?"

"I have to have some secrets," said Marita.

Indeed I must keep some secrets, she thought. *Especially the secret that while the court clerk did owe me a favor, she still does. The simplest solution was to win the case, and with a crowd of common people, Marita, street urchin become noble heiress, is the master.*

But it was worrisome. She'd counted on winning five to two!

GUARDING BOOKS

Stupidity is its own punishment; intelligence its own reward.

— *St. Ilra of Kallasia*

"Books!" muttered Bryan. "I'm hanging from this rope to get books."

Bryan was a professional caravan guard, used to crossing these mountains with expensive cargoes. Generally, he expected substantial bonuses for ensuring the safe passage of his employer's goods. The bonuses were guaranteed by the sale of the expensive cargo.

But times were hard, fewer and fewer caravans crossed the mountains, and bonuses were smaller and smaller. If it weren't for that, he would never have taken employment with a woman. She'd said her cargo was valuable, and she'd offered good rates —exceptionally good in these poor economic times. As a result, Bryan was leading a team of half a dozen guards and they were guarding a train of mules loaded with bags and boxes.

Then in the worst part of the pass a mule's load had slipped, and one of the bags came loose. It was incompetent cargo handling, or perhaps even an attempt to sabotage the train and allow a robbery. But he couldn't convince Lady Ilra of the danger. He couldn't convince her that her life and the rest of her possessions were more valuable than a single sack of goods.

He had even asked her what she would have done if the bag had fallen all the way into the canyon. "Use a longer rope," had been her quick answer.

So here he was, most of a rope length down the cliff, desperately trying to manage the rope and grab the sack that was lying on the ledge. Then through the partially loose mouth of the sack he identified the contents. Books! Each carefully wrapped in what looked like water resistant, oiled paper.

His first impulse was to shove the sack off the cliff and let it fall the rest of the way. But then he looked up to the point where his rope ended on the path, and she was looking down at him. She was a small woman, easy for him to defeat, he assumed, but she was up *there*, and he was down *here*, and she was holding a dagger. The message was clear. Send the sack up on the second rope, or I'll cut the one you're hanging from. He could only hope she meant that he'd be forced to take an additional length of rope and recover the books from the canyon floor.

So he carefully arranged himself so that he could hang from the rope and secure the sack, then tied it to the second rope. To add insult, she pulled the sack of books all the way up first, and only then allowed his men to bring him to the top of the cliff. It was humiliating to do this at a woman's command. It was insufferable to do it for books.

As they reloaded the mule, watching the cargo-master secure the load correctly, two of his men whispered in his ear.

"We've figured out that we are guarding books," they said. "We're agreed that we shouldn't have to risk our lives for that."

"We need the money," he pointed out.

"Well, we can kill her, dump the books, and keep the money she has already paid. We only have her word that there is any more money awaiting us at the end of this journey."

"Very well, I'll demand double our pay, and when she refuses, we'll dump her. That will provide a good story for any future employers."

Ilra had watched the men very carefully, but subtly, and she fully expected what was about to happen.

"The men are not happy to be guarding books," said Bryan.

"What difference does it make to you, so long as you are paid?"

"That's just it. How do we know we will be paid? We assumed you had a valuable cargo, and that would assure our payment when sold at the end of the journey."

"I have the money ready for you at journey's end."

"That's not enough."

"Oh? You demand double your pay, and half of the extra now."

Bryan tried to hide his surprise at her accurate guess. Why hadn't *he* thought of demanding half of the extra pay now?

"For double the pay, we'll guard your books, humiliating as it is."

She didn't so much stand up, as spring into a standing position, with a rapier in her hand. "You really should have thought of asking for half your extra pay immediately," she said. "You aren't very bright."

He reached for his sword, stung by the insult, angered at the way she intimidated him. How stupid could she be, thinking that a woman 5' 2" with a rapier could fight someone 6' 1" and more than double her weight—all of *his* weight being muscle!

There was movement, so quick he wasn't certain what had happened. His hand stung, and in surprise he lost hold of his sword. It clattered to the ground and came to a stop, precariously perched on the edge of the path. He was disarmed. By the time he realized that, her rapier was at his throat.

The men behind maneuvered for position, but it was simply not possible to edge by the two leaders in order to join the fight. It was between Bryan and Ilra.

"For what I paid you," said Ilra, "you will guard my books across the mountains. For your stupidity, you forfeit the second half of your pay, but I may, just *may*, restore it if you do an exceptional job the rest of the way."

"But lady, why take so much risk for books?"

"You think my books are useless, do you?"

"You can't eat them, you can't sell them. I'm a practical man. I like things that work."

"Interesting, then, that you are standing there unarmed, while I, a woman and a bookworm have you at my mercy. One might almost think I was the more practical person!"

"Let's see," she continued. "I knew what you were going to propose because I know how to read lips, a technique I learned from a book. It's loaded on the left hand side of the fourth mule. I know where it is by a memory technique I learned in another book, this one on the right hand side of the fifth mule."

"You are disarmed using a technique I learned from another useless book, designed to teach people who are smaller than average how to use techniques that give them the advantage over large boneheads such as yourself. You believe that I will be unable to sell any of my books, and most of them I don't actually want to sell, but some of them I do. I know who will pay for them, and how much, because of information I found in another one of those useless books. One of those bags of books toward the rear is worth about 5,000 silver crowns at our destination."

"But I also have an arrangement with a banker there so that I have much more at my disposal than the miserable pittance I'm paying you for this passage even without selling any books. I learned how to make such arrangements by reading these useless books."

"Most important to you right now, however, is the fact that another book back there teaches one techniques with the rapier. I could, of course, simply drive the rapier into your throat and you would fall dead. You think your men would then kill me, but because I've spent my time reading stupid, worthless books, I know better. Instead, I could do this"—she removed a button from his shirt right over his heart with a flick of the rapier —"and with a slight modification you would be bleeding to death. That weapon belt, which bears the throwing daggers you're hoping to reach for is easily dealt with as well"--with a another flick the belt was cut through and fell to the ground.

"My question is this," she said. "Would you rather die here and now, or would you rather guard this train the rest of its way to its destination and recover your pay?"

Fighting fury and terror in equal measures, Bryan grated out, "I'll see to it that you make it."

"I know what you're thinking. You're thinking you'll catch me asleep and kill me later. But another book back there has taught me about traps and alarms—deadly traps. Do you know that I know how to make at least 15 different poisons with materials we have with us, each of which could kill you and all your men?" It was her first lie, but it was a necessary one.

"We'll serve you well, lady," said a defeated Bryan.

And so the caravan of useless books continued on its way through the mountains, and reached its destination.

Birth of a Religion

Friendship is the worst enemy of justice, and its best friend.

— Folk Saying

Marat, priestess of Utu, adjusted her position until she had a clear shot both at the priest of Velanac, and at the drummers who stood to either side. To her left, she could see Amrar, priest of Ra, also prepared with a short bow, not all that different from hers. She stifled a laugh. *It's probably a minute or so before midnight out in the real world above, though I can't tell in this cave,* she thought. *I can barely move, my magical strength is expended, all my healing items, herbs, and other mixtures are empty. I'm bandaged around the chest, on one leg, and both arms. Pulling this bow is going to be painful. It's a fitting end to my career.*

Somewhere to her left, she knew that her friend, no colleague, no, it would be better to say *associate,* Natisha, was sneaking around the edge of the cavern. Just out of sight of the entrance stood the Lord Kaltros, leader of this little expedition, along with the three remaining hired guards. A few meters behind them would be Lord Mayor Zirdan, mayor of Sidroc, who was the expedition's patron. He was lying on a stretcher after being hit by several crossbow bolts in their last encounter. It was miraculous that, without any remaining priestly healing ability in the party, he was still alive.

With everyone injured in some way, it seemed likely that this would be the end. The only surprise was the absence of guards to stop them from getting into position to attack the high priest, but she wasn't going to complain about that. Perhaps they could at least interrupt whatever ritual he was performing before they all died in the inevitable counterattack.

She watched tensely for the moment when Natisha would be spotted. Natisha was, in her view, the expedition's thief, present for the purpose of opening doors, seeking out tricks and traps, and scouting. Kaltros called her their "tactical specialist," a title Marat was sure was designed to allow him to imagine he had not hired a common thief. Kaltros disliked common people generally, and thieves in particular, but he was also practical. Any moment now there would be a shout, and it would be her job to put an arrow through the high priest, with Amrar as backup.

Suddenly she saw movement directly behind the priest, inside his shrine. She saw Natisha bringing her sword down from above the priests head, but at the same time she noticed that his body was already cut in half, presumably from an upswing. The thief had made it all the way into the shrine and attacked the priest from behind. Marat released just as Natisha's sword descended, taking the drummer on her right. Amrar's arrow left a couple of seconds later and took the guard on the left. At least their agreement was still working. In the absence of a previously chosen target, he worked left and she worked right.

The drumming, stopped. Both shots were apparently fatal, almost certainly indicating that the drummers had not been armored, and perhaps had not been warriors at all. She and Amrar were reasonably good archers, but not *that* good. As the silence fell, Marat began to hear the background sounds. There was no clash of arms, no battle shouts. Instead she heard cries of terror, weeping, and confusion. She pulled herself farther along the ledge and looked down. There would be no counterattack. Gathered in the center of the room were the women and children of the cavern community, including in their ranks Kal, Half-Kal, Tlazil, and even an Avim child or two. There wasn't a warrior left. Though the women of the Half-Kal, Avim, and

Tlazil fought, and indeed they had met a number of them on their way in, the ones that were left were either old, wounded, or simply not qualified to fight.

Two guards went back to fetch the mayor, and then all gathered in the cavern. After some checking, they became certain that this was, indeed, the end of the road. The Temple of Velanac and the community that supported it were now destroyed.

"Oh, well," said Natisha, "Not much sport but I guess we need to finish the job." She drew her sword.

Phrases flashed through Marat's mind. *Father to the widow and the orphan. Help for the helpless. Sees everything. Avenges the poor.* "Stop!" she said.

Natisha looked amused, rather than angry. "I suppose you want them for your vermin collection," she said, combining a sneer and a sort of tolerant humor in the sound of her voice. "Vermin collection" was what Natisha called the shelter and orphanage at the temple back in Sidroc.

Natisha turned to the mayor. "What is to be done? We really haven't wiped this community out while they're alive. They'll be a lot of trouble to take home, and they'll cause trouble if we leave them." Her tone conveyed the sense of explaining the obvious to an idiot.

The mayor turned to Kaltros and shrugged his shoulders. Amongst these people he knew his only authority was based on his office, and with this group, that could make little difference. Kaltros hesitated.

"I agree with Marat," said Amrar. "We cannot kill them now. It would be wrong." His voice was flat. She never could tell what he was thinking, he was so unemotional. She had thought their two religions held similar moral views, but had been unable to be certain throughout this mission. Now the first time there was a disagreement in the team he was on her side.

"You two are the ones who care, you arrange to move them safely." Kaltros turned and started talking to the hired guards as soon as he'd said this, obviously dismissing the subject from his mind.

It was several days after they got back that Marat was called into her superior's office in Sidroc.

"I need you to make another trip to the south and establish shrines. We have two acolytes ready for ordination as priests and three additional acolytes we can put on independent assignment. You'll check these villages every so often and supervise them. The villages need good moral instruction and a strong temple presence or the Velanac people will take over again."

"What about the temples of Ra?" asked Marat.

"What about them?"

"They also plan to establish a presence. Perhaps we should cooperate, put our acolytes where their priests are, and so forth. It would provide for mutual defense, and their priests could help with the instruction." Marat felt this suggestion was only reasonable.

"Place our acolytes under the guidance of the heathen priests of Ra?" yelled Arad. "I'm senior priest of Utu on this entire continent, and we *will* keep this religion pure."

"But their moral tenets are almost identical to ours!" exclaimed Marat. She knew she should have known better, but she simply couldn't stop herself. The solution to the lack of trained priests was simply too obvious.

"You're on probation," said Arad decisively. He was angry now, and worried. He wanted this problem behind him and was going to have no discussion. "Begin preparations for your trip. You will follow my directions exactly in this. If you disobey me, I'll excommunicate you."

The words struck Marat like hammer blows. Excommunicate? There were only a couple hundred followers of their faith on this continent. She was the junior partner, but nonetheless she was a partner, her boss's right hand. How could this seem so right to her and so wrong to her high priest?

Marat left, heading to the downtown area to purchase supplies in preparation for her trip, but her heart wasn't in it. She had been so certain. Perhaps it was because she was a descendant of the Enzar, half Galiru and half human, but steeped in the Enzar way of thinking. Tradition was much less important to her.

"Hey! Watch where you're going, Marat! One would think you weren't paying any attention." Amrar's voice was as dry as ever, but there was a slight smile playing around his lips.

"I was thinking about something else," she said.

"How about a drink?"

They entered *The Broken Lantern*, a bar that catered to the middle class of Sidroc, to the extent that there was a middle class there. Marat poured out her heart to Amrar, the possibilities she had seen, and what could be done for the moral growth of this country with the sort of cooperation she was proposing.

"Why not make a cooperative temple the way the Enzar do?" suggested Amrar.

"Cooperative Temple?"

"Yes, cooperative. All the priests support all the gods and learn all the rituals. Worshipers either give their allegiance to the temple itself, or to the specific god, but worship that god at the temple."

"An ecumenical temple, the Ecumenical Temples of the Sun." This was exciting! What couldn't they do with this?

"You have a way with words." Amrar was clearly pleased with the idea. "Why don't we do it?"

"How can I? The High Priest is opposed."

"Well, we're using Enzar tradition to establish the temple, but our religions are both Ardenean. What's the Ardenean tradition for dissident priests?"

"Well, you generally start a new branch of the religion."

"Why not do that here?"

"But there are only a couple hundred of us!"

"True, but first I want to ask you who has more contact with those members, you, or your High Priest?"

Marat stared at the ceiling for a couple of minutes. "I think they look to me. In fact, I teach almost all the classes for the acolytes as well."

"So once you're established, all of those members, acolytes, and priests will have to make a choice. At the same time, you'll have the support of all of my temples as well. My organization is actually smaller, but combined with the portion of yours that will follow you, we'll have the basis for a strong movement."

Marat sat alone in the shrine of her apartment. She was already late in returning to the temple to begin preparations to leave on the expedition she'd been order to lead. She hoped her High Priest hadn't yet noticed. The key to creating a dissident movement, she knew, was to do so before one was excommunicated. Excommunication meant starting over.

In front of her was a small altar, and in her hands were dice. Sacred dice for divination, six sides, odd numbers for "no," even for "yes." She set up for her questions:

Can I, as a priestess, establish this new religion? [6]

Will you, my god, honor this religion with your power? [4]

Will you honor the choice of existing priests to join with the new religion? [6]

Will you accept my consecration of this shrine as the first territory of the new religion? [6]

As she asked these questions, there was a similar scene in the Sidroc Temple of Utu:

Is Marat contemplating rebellion against my authority? [4]

Can she create an independent temple if I first excommunicate her? [3]

He immediately moved to the ritual of excommunication, the particular ritual used when the target was absent. Unfortunately for him, he completed the ritual just a little late. Marat had already declared herself an independent priestess of the new Ecumenical Temples of the Sun.

CONVENIENT TIMING

The new arrival joined the crowd in the bar of The Featherless Parrot, one of Shalem's business inns. What was meant by a "business inn" was simply a place where it was more likely that the patrons were making deals than that they were being entertained. It suited the visitor to be in such a place.

Those who watched him—and there were many—saw a youngish man with a slightly effeminate look. It was so obvious that he didn't really belong in this place that most assumed that he really did. Nobody could be as weak and inattentive as he looked, and yet alive, unless he was very competent indeed.

It was some time before anyone decided to contact the visitor. Making contact with a stranger in a business bar could be dangerous, though this one didn't look like he was waiting for anyone in particular. He seemed to be just enjoying a drink and some dinner, as unlikely as that might be. It was possible he was looking to hire and was waiting for someone to contact him.

"Welcome to Shalem." The tone was not welcoming, but the visitor looked up into the face of a middle aged man.

"Really?" he said, with a slight twinkle in his eyes. "I kind of doubt it."

"Well, as welcome as anyone is here. Why are you here?" It was abrupt, but one approach was as good as another.

"I'm just looking around," said the visitor. "I'm in from Malethia via Aagerinar, security consultant to the East Coast Commercial Guild."

It was a little bit too much information, but it fit with the careless and incompetent attitude. It indicated confidence. And one who claimed to represent the East Coast Commercial Guild would have the necessary backing, assuming he really did represent them.

"Do you need any information?" asked the local. This would be seen as an obvious offer to sell, as no information was free in Shalem.

"Perhaps." The visitor paused. "And perhaps I can provide some in exchange."

"What would you like to know?"

"I'm looking for a tolerably reliable source of guards, not too expensive. The tasks will not be excessively demanding and the potential rewards reasonable." The visitor did not seem to mind putting his cards on the table. "What would you like in exchange for giving me a rundown of the potential sources? I'll understand if you give better than normal recommendations for your own organization."

"What do you have?" asked the local, wondering how the visitor could know that he represented potential people for hire. Then he recalled that this would be the most common reason someone would approach a lone individual in a business bar. It just wasn't usually done with this little preparation.

"Well, I have some good information, useless to me, but perhaps of interest to someone here. I would exchange that information for a good rundown on mercenary organizations. I would be very annoyed, however, if your information did not prove as valuable as mine."

"And I if yours is not, or is not exclusive."

"I think you can count on exclusivity. The value of the information could be quite high, provided you know how to manage it."

There was a considerable space around them now, as people who didn't want to appear involved moved aside, and thus removed the cover for those who would dearly have loved to hear the conversation. The inn's manager cursed as he realized that the entire conversation was taking place too far from any of his listening holes for him to get even the gist of what was going on. Nobody sat in the middle of the room for such a conversation!

"Very well," said the local. "What's more, I'll go first, but I expect value!"

There were several minutes of conversation, with the local doing most of the talking, and the visitor occasionally nodding or asking brief questions. The local was convinced that he was talking to the real thing, that this person was indeed who he said he was. He was glad he actually knew something about hiring guards, and he gave information he was certain would not get him caught.

When the visitor was satisfied, he said, "OK, here's your information in payment. I came here on the Serinon, based out of Uligar, which I joined in Malethia. They made a stop in Aagerinar harbor, where I had some contact, let us say with an individual in a bar like this—always allowing that Aagerinar has no bars quite like this."

"What my contact told me was that Marita, heir to the Earl Northmarch, and also third in line for the Duchy of Aagerinar, is coming here on an official visit, or at least as official a visit as one makes to Shalem."

The local started to interrupt, but the visitor raised a hand slightly and he stopped.

"You're about to tell me that this is already well-known. And indeed it is. It is so well-known that a visitor newly arrived like myself already knows that it is well-known. What is much less known, and indeed seems to be practically unknown here, is that Marita is not on speaking terms with her father, or with the duke, though she is good friends with the ducal heir, Alexander. The reason for this is that she is rumored to have killed in the neighborhood of 17 people, and she is a suspect in perhaps as many robberies. She was actually tried for murder but was not convicted. The claim is that she's only 17 years old, but nobody knows precisely where she was born or when. She is adopted, you know."

The local didn't know, but he nodded.

"My contact believes that she is, in fact, an operative of Aagerinar intelligence, and carries out her activities on behalf of the government. In addition, he has good reason to believe that she is coming to Shalem for the purpose of killing Lucius, head of family Grunder, in retaliation for his killing of an Aagerinar shipmaster last month. Aagerinar authorities believe the killing was done simply to avoid paying a bill, and the authorities here, as we both know, would never convict a head of one of the commercial families."

"And how do I know you are telling the truth?" asked the local.

A look of contempt came over the visitor's face. "If you can't judge what I say by now, you don't deserve your job. Decide quickly!"

The local could not really be sure. He wasn't entirely sure how the visitor expected him to be able to judge such intelligence so quickly, yet the visitor seemed so confident! He didn't want to appear to be a fool or incompetent, and he wasn't sure that he would be able to deal with the results if the visitor became angry, so he decided to accept the information. His customers could judge its value for themselves. He would have to think of ways to present it that would make it appear more definite!

Lucius joined Marita for a dance at the reception put on by the Aagerinar commercial representative. He was uncomfortable being there in the first place, knowing not only that he had killed the master of an Aagerinar registered ship, but that the Aagerinar authorities believed he was the culprit. Then had come the message that this very young lady was here to kill him in retaliation. The more he thought about the presentation of that message, the less he could find of substance to support it. Nonetheless, he would appear weak if he refused the invitation and even weaker still if he refused to dance with the guest of honor.

She looked 17, she talked like a 17 year old, she seemed to be an empty headed moron of a noble. The only reason she would be accused of theft or murder just had to be convenience. Yet now, at the moment when he should be feeling reassurance, he was becoming even more certain that she was here to kill him. When their eyes met, he simply became sure that she knew who he was, what he had done, and that she meant him to die for it. He was glad he'd hired extra guards. When he got home, he would double his guard again. Nobody would get within a kilometer of his home. He would be surrounded by guards whenever he moved.

Later, he watched again as she danced with the sergeant who had come with his additional guard detail. He'd asked the man to size her up and let him know.

He would have been interested in a conversation between the sergeant and one of his men, as the sergeant commented that Marita had mentioned a number of difficulties Lucius had experienced in paying employees in full in a timely manner. Her off-hand comments had shaken him up. The trooper himself had heard similar rumors in the town. Would they get their pay? Would they even survive that long? Mentally, they began to compare their positions with those of the regular guards. They discovered that they were generally in the open or in temporary positions, while the regular guards were in well-prepared and well-concealed positions.

The assassin was positioned on the south wall, just in view of the guardhouse at the front of the building. It had been trivially easy to get into position, one that was just above a household guard position. Sharp eyes watched until the captain of the hired guards appeared, and then a single crossbow bold through the neck killed him instantly. What was clear to the other guards at the front gate was that the bolt had come from the direction of a household guard position.

This was it! This was how Lucius avoided payment! The pattern was repeating itself. Immediately they began to fire back.

Lucius heard the fighting start and turned to his own chief of security. It took him only seconds to think it through. It had all been a trap. False information about someone coming to kill him forces him to hire new guards. The new guards are actually in someone else's pay, and they are the ones actually hired to kill him. He didn't pause long enough to think about how his enemies had arranged to get him to hire just the right guards.

"Go!" he yelled to the chief of security. "Kill them all!"

The assassin fairly glided through the battle. Everyone was so busy chasing one another that they had no time to notice another invader. Occasionally a guard got in the way, and it was necessary to pause to put a crossbow bolt in just the right place, or employ a quick thrust with a sword.

It ended in the office of Lucius, head of the Grunder family. As the door slid open, as several traps designed for his security were sprung, but somehow did not touch the assassin, he knew that he had been played. As his eyes met those of his nemesis for a moment just before the assassin plunged a dagger into his heart, the full realization dawned.

A few minutes sufficed to empty the safe of easily transportable items. The battle was still going on as the assassin left.

Marita, reputed playgirl, thief, and assassin boarded her ship and left the city the next day. Hundreds of witnesses said she could not possibly have had anything to do with the battle and the death of Lucius, head of family Grunder.

She had just happened to be present again at the wrong time and place.

WHO WILL PROTECT US?

Our frenzied packing was interrupted by the arrival of the royal messenger.

"Good news!" he said. "There's a cease fire. You don't have to leave."

We all stood around watching him, foolishly holding precious possessions in our arms, and looking at the wagons, mules and donkeys that were partially loaded.

"What happened?" I asked.

"A cease fire," he repeated helpfully, spurring his horse. Then he stopped and wheeled around. "Oh," he added, "it wouldn't have done you any good to run. The giants are already northeast of here and were moving around your village to cut off the impies to the south." He nodded as though thoroughly satisfied with this speech, then spurred his horse again and was gone.

I had noted the Eselena Royal uniform, but many of the villagers had not. "Impies?" they asked. "Should he call the imperial troops impies?"

"We always did in the Guard," I tell them. The Eselena Royal Guard had a proud tradition. Proud, that is, other than having been conquered by the Ardenean Empire several centuries back. We had always thought ourselves more disciplined than the imperial troops. Man for man we were more than a match for them. Too bad they had about 100 men for each of ours! But independence was so long lost as to be a legend, and the Eselena

Royal Guard had fought for the empire alongside those impies proudly and well.

I watched uncertainly as villagers began to unpack and return wagons, donkeys and mules to their usual places. It was only three days since we'd first realized a war had started. A young royal had ridden into the village, tired, dirty and wounded.

"Giants pouring across the border," he'd gasped.

"Why?" was the question on everyone's lips.

"Because they don't like us!" he said.

I was called upon to tend his wounds. People assumed that someone retired from the royals (the army, they called it) would know how to tend wounds. I didn't mind. It gave me a chance to question him.

"I'm to take a message to our headquarters, get reinforcements," he told me.

"Is it true it was unprovoked?" I asked. It had been many years since the giants had attacked, and normally the wars were started by our people, not by them. Every so often someone on the imperial staff would decide the giants of Kachadahz were a threat which should be dealt with proactively and off would go an army to attack. And back would come a bedraggled army much smaller than when it had left. But the giants never pursued them very far before they tired of the chase and went home.

"Well, no, not exactly," he replied.

"How 'not exactly'?" I asked. "One either provokes or one doesn't, it would seem!"

"Well, you know about the invasion of Sinedan, don't you?" he asked.

I didn't. I had an idea that Sinedan was off to the east.

"We decided to take back Sinedan. Most of the reserves were sent in that direction for the invasion. I'm going to ask for reserves, but I know that they aren't there. What we have left is 200 kilometers behind the front lines. But as for provocation, Kachadahz reacted badly to the invasion. They sent forces into Arden to attack our flank. Some idiot of a general or another ordered an attack on the border by the impy border guards, reinforced, he assumed, by mobile reserve units, the ones 200 kilometers from here. You can guess what happened then!"

"And the giants are pursuing?" I asked. It was doctrine that the giants couldn't keep their concentration long enough to take much territory.

"I don't know how far, but they're organized," he replied. "They didn't break under charge or heavy crossbow fire. They held their line and rained arrows on us. With their bows, if they do that, we're nearly helpless. Our casualties were staggering. I barely escaped with my messages."

I didn't feel the need to interrogate him further, but I had gone immediately to the village headman and told him to warn people to be ready to move. In my day it had been doctrine that the giants wouldn't pursue for long, that they hadn't the patience to sustain a barrage of giant longbow fire, and that a determined cavalry charge would either spook them, or provoke them into a loose charge. Their firepower, combined with organization was too frightening to contemplate.

Just as ordering border guards to attack them was too stupid to contemplate.

But the young soldier's eyes spoke truth.

Then had come the ragged bands of troops running ahead of the giants. That was two days later. The retreat was pretty much at the forced march pace. The fleeing troops didn't say much, except to demand supplies and then continue to run. What could we do about it? We had no weapons. By the time the stragglers had all vanished to the north, we had few supplies left. Fortunately they had not found everything.

So we were happy not to run, but surprised at the cease-fire. Another doctrine had always been: "You can't negotiate with Kachadahz." But apparently one could!

That night some horsemen rode into town. They rode in from the north, looking fresh and well kept. They obviously hadn't been in the fighting. There were about 80 of them, looking fine in decorated uniforms. I wondered if they had ever seen combat!

Their captain called our headman out of his house. No respect to his rank, age or position. He demanded housing and food. "We're here to protect you," he said as though that were an intolerable imposition on his time. "It's only right that you take proper care of us."

So we offered them such shelter as we had. What else could we do? We offered them such food as we had left, and little enough there was of it.

They weren't satisfied. They said they must be properly fed to defend us. They announced that we were likely treasonous traitors (their redundancy) and that they would have the food out of us. Then they organized a search of the village. When it was done, they had what was left of our food.

They returned to the village square where they were holding the headman. Faster than anyone could respond, they threw a noose around his neck and the rope over a tree branch and hoisted him slowly off the ground, not so his neck would be broken but so that he would strangle.

The captain announced: "That is what happens to traitors who try to hide needed supplies from the troops in time of war."

Technically, he was correct. Concealing needed supplies was a crime and could be considered treason. Likely, I thought, he can get by with this. Who are we here in this village? Who in the imperial government will care about us? A little shading of the facts and we were all collaborators.

The captain announced that he was in charge and the village was under martial law. "Anyone else who tries to hinder us in our duties will meet the same fate." The headman was not dead yet. He was going to die slowly.

It was not until evening that the screaming started. I don't know in which house. But I realized what was happening and stepped out to look around. The troops were lounging around the village. Apparently they were not concerned about legality. You could hang traitors, but you couldn't rape the women or kill just anyone. I could see the body of our headman still hanging in the tree. In the door of one house, I recognized our blacksmith fallen across his own threshold. He looked dead. The exits from the village were guarded.

To the northeast I could see a fire. It looked like a large one. The enemy camp? Very likely.

I huddled in my hut, feeling the shame. I, the sole warrior of the village, too old and slow to do anything about what was happening. Would they kill all the witnesses? Would we all die?

There was a scraping at my back window. I went and pulled aside the board that blocked it. Outside was the blacksmith's wife.

"You must do something," she whispered. Then she held her finger to her mouth. "They're not letting us move around any more," she continued.

"What can I do?" I asked. "I'm old. I couldn't fight you, much less those soldiers out there."

"You can go to the camp," she replied.

"What camp?" Then it dawned on me. "You mean the giants' camp?" I was stunned. One didn't ask the giants of Kachadahz for anything. If one asked, one didn't get it. Or perhaps one got killed for one's pains. It just wasn't done.

"The giants' camp," she confirmed.

"They won't help us. You'd better put your hope in the arrival of higher ranking officers or a unit that respects the law."

"There won't be any," she said with conviction. "The captain told me we were at his mercy for several months. He seemed pretty happy."

I thought about it. The giants were pursuing. The giants were negotiating. But still, I couldn't go ask the giants for help!

"They raped my Mona; they killed my husband when he tried to protect her," she said. "Anything would be better than this!"

I couldn't argue with her on that. The giants weren't known for casual killing or for raping human women. Actually, they'd rarely had the chance.

"What do the other people think?" I stalled.

"How am I supposed to find out?" she asked.

There was a bellow from the direction of her house. I could see her back yard from my hut. A soldier was in the yard looking around. She broke and ran toward him. He knocked her to the ground and then dragged her back toward the house by her collar. I knew what would happen.

"Can an old soldier still do anything?" I asked myself. Certainly I couldn't fight, but could I sneak past the guards. Were the giants a better option for the village than what we had? I saw the headman hanging in the tree. I saw the body of the blacksmith, guilty only of protecting his daughter, lying dead on his own doorstep. I saw again the arrogant look in the eyes of the young captain. Somehow I knew that nothing could be worse than months of living in a village where he was the law.

I grabbed my knife and checked myself over for any obvious effort I could make at concealment. The years out of the royals had loosened some of my careful grooming. I was dusty and dirty enough to move around in the dark. Things were as good as they were going to get.

I climbed out the back window, and started sneaking toward the edge of town. Slowly I made my way from cover to cover. We didn't have a wall, only a palisade of poles. I knew where I could slip out, provided there was no guard there. As I approached the wall, I heard an exclamation. One of the impies!

"Did you hear something?" I heard him say.

"No," said another voice.

"I think I did," he said.

I huddled even deeper into the cover I'd found, wishing myself smaller and invisible.

He nearly stepped on me. He was drunk. I could smell his breath even from my hiding place on the ground with him standing. Finally, he turned and left me. He and his companion walked back further into the village.

I made my move. Slowly, up to the fence, then quickly through the hole I knew was there, then out onto the plain.

It was painful to crawl. My old joints didn't appreciate crawling close to the ground, but there was no cover. I had to get hundreds of meters away from the village before I would feel safe to stand and walk normally. At one point I thought I heard a crossbow bolt fired from the town, but I couldn't be sure. I just kept on moving.

I went toward the supposed giant camp. Now it occurred to me that I didn't really know it was a giant camp. I just assumed it was. But as I approached I soon knew for certain. I decided that there was no point in sneaking. I'd just walk up to the camp and let them spot me. I'd see what they did.

I wasn't far from the camp when I heard a whistle. Further up the path a giant jumped up at the whistle and looked my way. It took him some time to spot me. Then he came toward me, looked me over carefully and said, "What have we here?"

I said, "I am Karano, from the village of Buyul. I have come to ask your aid."

"Our aid?" he said doubtfully. But he didn't laugh.

"Yes, we need help. The imperial troops have come and killed our headman and they are raping our women." I paused and watched his face. His expression didn't change.

"So?" he shrugged slightly. His face slowly changed into what I took to be a puzzled look.

"I have nowhere else to turn!" I told him.

"But that is imperial territory. We agreed not to take it. You want us to invade the empire again." He said all this very slowly, almost as though he wasn't sure what it meant. Though he obviously *was* sure.

He paused, shook his head, and stared at me some more.

"I think you need to see the commander," he said. "Come!"

I followed him. The commander was just about the largest giant I had ever seen, with a fine suit of armor, a giant longbow nearby, a very expensive looking giant sword, and a barrel (from my perspective) of ale held in both hands. Casually sprawled on the ground near him was a human girl, in her late teens I guessed. Her only weapon was a dagger, but she looked more vigorous and efficient than decorative.

Several more giants were either sprawled around the area or standing watch around the camp. A couple of Ertzlu, dressed in Greenhaven style clothing which I still recognized, were sitting on a log, also near the commander giant. I knew this group of giants could take care of the force in our village easily, if they wanted to.

I repeated my tale.

"You're asking me to invade some more, eh?" he asked.

He looked faintly amused.

The girl said something in a foreign language. We'd been speaking imperial standard. I didn't even recognize the language. He gave a bark of laughter and then said something more in the same language. She made a gesture at him that, from the look on her face, I took to be obscene. Another bark of laughter.

He turned back to me. "Because this most beautiful of human females (obscene gesture from the girl) wishes me to save your helpless human females, and because I generally dislike all things imperial, I will save your village."

He hollered an order. Giants dropped barrels of ale, grabbed weapons and went on alert. A few more curt gestures and commands and they all took off running in different directions. A more confused scene I would have trouble imagining! Some time during all this, the two Ertzlu disappeared.

The girl startled me by touching my shoulder. "Come along grandpa," she said in faintly accented imperial standard. "Let's go watch the fun, or at least as much of it as won't be over before we can get there."

She had thrown a leather shirt on and grabbed a staff. I saw that besides her dagger, she had a small hand crossbow. She must be a priestess of some sort, but damned if I could remember more the names of any of those foreign gods.

We walked slowly, at my pace. I was surprised that the giants, considering that they had a priestess, were willing to go into battle without her.

By the time we got to the village it was all over. In the town square, the imperial troops were standing in a group in the square. Several of them were dead in the streets. The captain was being held immobile.

The young priestess ordered us all to go to bed and stay out of the streets.

The next morning, we were all called to the square. The giant was sitting on a large, improvised chair. Before him stood the captain of the imperial company. The priestess brought several witnesses from the town and led them through testimony about what the troops had done. At the end, she asked the captain if he had anything he wanted to say. He started in with a speech about this being imperial territory, him being the law, and the giants being invaders.

The giant held up his hand. "I'm a *successful* invader and you're scum," he said. He flicked his fingers at the captain and three giants grabbed him and started to beat him up and kick him through the street. While this performance was going on, the next imperial soldier was brought forward. As the blacksmith's wife got up to accuse him of murder and rape he fell on his face and began to plead for mercy. A flick of the giant's fingers and he joined his captain in the street. I imagined that the captain could no longer be alive, but the giants were still playing with his body.

I'm afraid it horrified me more than what the imperial troops had done at the time. Afterward, when I wasn't watching, I started to feel a sense of justice in it. Most of the village had not even been disgusted when the giants were kicking the evildoers through the streets. They cheered! I understood how they felt, even through my revulsion.

All those who had personally participated in any of the atrocities of rape or murder were executed in the same manner. Some who had only played a peripheral role were beaten less severely. All were disarmed and sent from the village. The giant commander took over. To us, he was a friend.

It was two days later that a lieutenant in royal uniform with a small cavalry patrol approached the town. He signaled a parley. All he wanted to do, however, was read a royal decree.

Eselena declared itself independent of the Ardenean Empire, it said. Eselena had officially requested the protection of Kachadahz from the depredations of imperial troops. The Kachadahz government having granted this request, all royal Kachadahz and allied forces were permitted to operate freely in our territory, and all officials of the Eselena government and its subordinate chartered entities should cooperate in every way with duly constituted Kachadahz authority.

Then he and the giant shook hands. And he and the priestess. A while later he found me. "Grandpa," he said, "you saved this village."

"I suppose I did," I replied.

"Everything will be OK now," he said.

"You're sure?" I asked. "What will these giants do with what they've taken?"

"I don't know," he said, "but it sure can't be worse than what the imperials did to us."

I thought I'd heard that somewhere before.

CARAVAN STOP

The Jevlir Caravansary is just across the river from the small, but well-fortified town of Jevlir. Immediately to the west, the great east-west caravan route enters the pass of the mountains, variously known as the East Enzar range, Malkuthim range, or God's Backbone. The ancient road once led from sea to sea, and theoretically still does, though nobody can recall anyone making such a journey.

Theoretically also, Jevlir's mayor and town council owe their allegiance to the baron (who has more variants to his title than the mountains have names), who in turn theoretically owes his allegiance to the Duke, resident in Aagerinar, far to the east. At the time of our story, the baron is only marginally aware of the name of the duke (Alexander II), and rather than giving allegiance to any hereditary noble, the various members of the town council are owned by different merchant houses, and it is rumored that some are owned by bandit chiefs. It is also rumored that some town council members are owned by more than one person.

Caravans come to the caravansary and generally spend just one night. If they are headed east, to Aagerinar, they will leave their extra guards here, and proceed with only reasonable security. Unreasonably tense security is the rule in the mountains. If they are headed west, they will hire some of the guards that others have released. There are guards who spend their entire careers guarding caravans along this route. The pay is good for any who survive. Occasionally someone even survives long enough to retire, and the Caravan Guards Guild pays a handsome pension to any who make it, though survival to retirement is so rare that the total pension payments form only a small part of the guild's budget..

Next to the caravansary, between it and the entry to the pass, there is the ruin of an Enzar temple. The building is at least 3,000 years old, though from the outside it looks nearly whole. Those who claim to have seen the inside–a very small number– say that it is completely gutted, and it looks like the stone itself has been burned away in places. Very few bother to investigate Enzar temples unless extremely large treasure is to be expected, and none of the folks who claim to have seen the inside appear to be rich. Thus the temple is avoided by all.

Just now, Jared, Lieutenant in the Ducal army of Alexander II, is standing outside the temple on the western side, looking at the body of his captain. The cause of his death was altogether mundane and obvious, apparently having nothing to do with taboos about the temple. A heavy crossbow bolt was stuck in his neck. All of this took less time to see than it does to describe, and Jared, along with the four soldiers who were with him dropped to the ground, presenting less of a target. It looked, however, as though the captain had been dead for at least a couple of hours. It was unlikely anyone was about to shoot them now.

Jared got to his knees and scanned the cliffs to the west. The entrance to the mountain pass was quite rugged, and there were many places to hide–too many to allow certainty about where the shooter must have been. Sending one guard north and one south, Jared called on his sergeant and the remaining guard to look around for anything obvious. All of the captain's equipment was still present. He had not been robbed. They found nothing else to indicate what had happened.

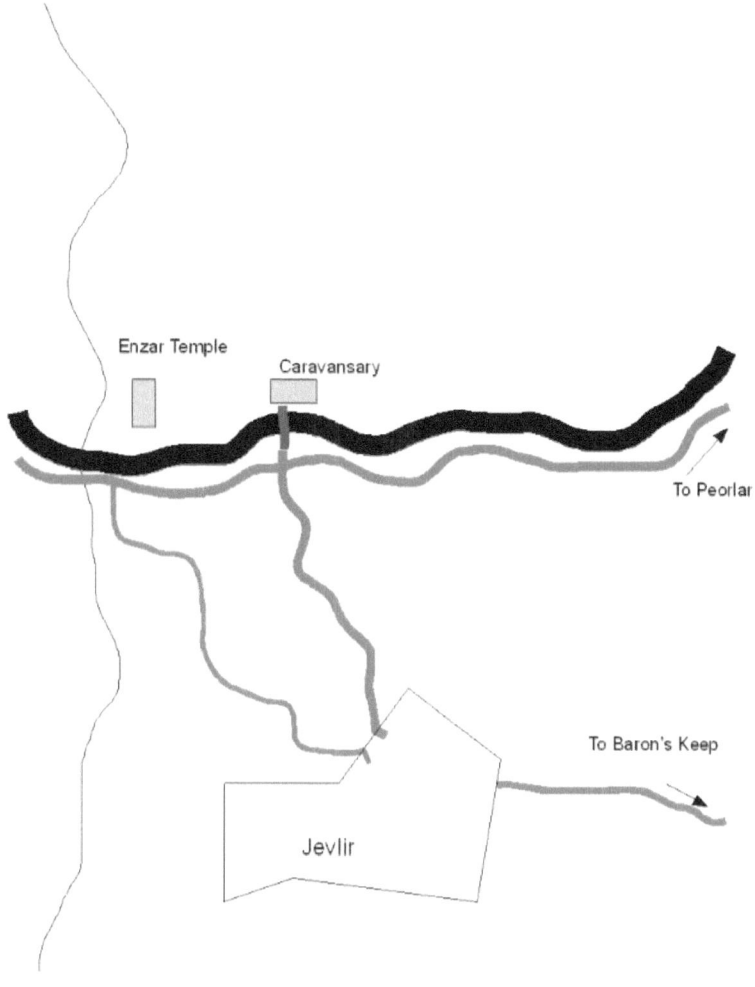

"Why was he in this location?" asked the sergeant quietly. It was a logical question. There seemed to be no good reason to expose oneself in what was probably the best position in the Jevlir area to make oneself a target for a crossbow bolt. With that thought they picked up the captain's body between them and moved him around to the northern side of the temple. It was not precisely a safe position, but at least it was a position where nobody had yet been shot today. The two guards followed.

When they got there, Jared looked at his sergeant. "I'll take two of the men and head downstream, staying on the northern side of the river. We'll cross back at Peorlar and go to the camp. You go back to the village and tell Lt. Qerelir to make a show of moving out of town and heading east. And remember, I don't want anyone who doesn't already know to suspect the captain is dead."

"One change, Lieutenant." The sergeants voice was respectful, but also determined. "You go back to town and get the company out. I will take the captain's body."

Jared was silent for a moment. Was it time to assert his authority? The sergeant was right. He was the best man to go back into town, while the sergeant could easily get the body to the required place. People would hardly believe the company was leaving on routine business if the sergeant came back and then they hurried off.

"Very well, sergeant, but be careful. Leave the crossbow bolt where it is. I want Qerelir to look at it."

In town Jared had to break the news to Qerelir, who was Kelaru, and thus regarded automatically as a much better woodsman. She was also older than he was and more experienced, but he still outranked her by days as a Lieutenant.

He needn't have worried about her reaction. As soon as he told her his plan, she went into action. The innkeeper was informed that folks who were occupying his courtyard were about to leave, that the captain had already headed out of town and the troops were obliged to follow. Soldiers started discussing what they would do when they got back to the big city. Jared was pretty certain none of them believed they were actually on their way home, but they put on a good show. He remembered this same group less than six months ago as they left on this mission, each quite skilled as warriors, but lacking teamwork. The captain had taught them to read one another and cooperate. Now it was paying off.

In less than an hour they were on the road. Once they were out of sight of Jevlir, Jared signaled Qerelir to join him. "The captain is dead," he explained.

She showed no sign of shock. "I was certain of it, and I'll bet half the troops know it too. But obviously you wanted to leave without people realizing that."

"Yes. I need you to look at the body. We found it between the temple and the mountains with a crossbow bolt through the neck. I need some idea of how he died."

"Did you say 'through the neck' as in the point sticking out?"

"Yes."

"That's odd. When you said he was north of the temple I immediately assumed sniper. A good heavy crossbow could just do it from the cliffs, but I doubt it would go all the way through. In fact, such a shot would risk failing to kill instantly, and the captain carried an excellent healing amulet, courtesy of the pretty priestess."

"Well, my initial question was why he was back there. But how could anyone get near enough with a cocked crossbow? There's no cover."

"Are you sure he was actually shot there?"

"We found nothing at all, but the ground is hard. There's no way to tell."

"Probably not." Was Jared just imagining that she was thinking she would have been able to tell?

"Do you know where the captain was going?"

"I think he was meeting his source at the caravansary. I have no idea whether he got there or not."

"When we get back, I'm going to have to go there and do it alone."

Qerelir looked at him for a few moments. He was afraid she was going to argue and suggest that he needed to take additional people along. It was essential that he do this all without getting noticed. But after staring at him a bit she just said, "OK."

As expected, there was no difficulty meeting with the sergeant and his men, and then the troops prepared to return to Jevlir, this time on the southern side of the river. A little ways east of the town they settled into a hidden campsite. It was hard to be certain nobody would come across them, but they were fairly safe.

Yaran was not the sort of person you really wanted to know. For one thing, he smelled bad. His clothes were dirty, he was generally drunk, and his speech was slurred and not terribly interesting. When anyone could manage to understand him, he was generally asking for money to buy more beer.

Yaran lived at the Caravansary. He did not live in it, but sort of at it and around it. He regularly moved from place to place, sometimes because he was ordered to get out, and sometimes just because he didn't want to stay in one place long enough to be noticed.

In the Caravansary Inn, designed to provide a bed, showers, and decent food for those merchants who could afford it, four men gathered around a table by the window. One of them looked out the window and saw Yaran there on the ground just outside.

"It's OK," he said to the others. "It's just the old drunk."

"Here's the deal," said the second man. "We have 6,000 silver valors to add to the pot if you will take care of him tonight. Remember, this is as important to you guys as it is to us. We just need the timing changed."

"What about the commandos?" asked the third.

"Don't worry about them," said the second, "I've arranged for them to be otherwise occupied. In fact, I believe they've all left town, which will make even that unnecessary. Just in case, however, I haven't canceled my little diversion. They won't fail to go to the aid of the pretty priestess." He chuckled.

"OK, go with it. He'll be coming into town tonight to meet with the young militia officers. You can do it after he leaves town on the way home."

"I prefer it during the dinner," said the second man.

"Do it however you want," said the first. "We can't allow him to continue cooperating with Aagerinar. None of us can. If the Duke's troops set up here permanently it will be bad for business."

Jared set out for the caravansary. He was not a foolhardy man, and he was not happy to be following the course that had probably led to his captain's death, but he needed the information that had gotten his captain killed. At least he expected that if the captain was contacting a source and then got killed, there was probably a connection.

It was after dark that he entered the caravansary grounds. It was impossible to approach the caravansary quietly and subtly, because one had to cross a long bridge across the river, and the bridge afforded no cover at all. Jared removed all insignia prior to crossing, and his normal clothing and armor did not distinguish him from the many caravan guards who were a common sight. Unless someone recognized him personally, he would be fine.

He handed his horse's reins to one of the stable boys and headed for the bar. He uttered the appropriate insult as he passed the form of the source, and knew that once he had taken time for a drink he would find the man in the stables. He needed that drink just now.

After a few minutes spent with some quite decent beer, Jared wandered slowly outside and sauntered over to the stable. He was still carrying his beer mug and looking rather casual. He stopped and checked on his own horse. Seeing that the fine animal was well cared for he continued down the line, finally finding an empty stall, and in the back, Yaran the drunk. Unknown to the regulars at the inn, this man was also Yaran the security agent, whose specialty was collecting information where others would be noticed. As he sniffed, Jared thought the agent played his part a bit too thoroughly

"What news?" he asked.

"You're not Porivinar," replied Yaran.

"Indeed I'm not. He was shot earlier today. That makes anything you know doubly important."

"It's a good thing I know you. If I didn't I wouldn't care how many passwords you claimed to have." He ignored the fact that no password had been offered, nor were any used in this area. Personal recognition was the standard. Yaran was just trying to put him off balance, an almost instinctive activity for him.

"Your news?" insisted Jared.

"Who shot the captain?"

"We don't know. Did you see him today?"

"No, and I was expecting to."

"What did you have for him."

"There is a plan tonight to assassinate the baron's heir, Jerard. The folks I heard didn't give a name, but he's coming into town tonight, and they think he cannot be permitted to keep cooperating with Aagerinar. That eliminates the old baron himself, who doesn't cooperate with anyone. So they're going to kill Jerard. They're planning a diversion at the Ecumenical Temple to distract you."

"That makes sense. But why kill the captain?"

"You said he was west of the temple, toward the mountains?"

"Yes."

"Did the crossbow bolt penetrate very far?"

"Yes. Qerelir already noted that. She thinks he was killed elsewhere, by somebody close."

"Porivinar would have seen anyone that close and would have defended himself—probably successfully."

"Unless he met someone he knew and trusted."

"Trusted? Hardly. Knew, possibly. Someone had only to offer him information and he'd make the meeting. On the other hand, he might have been surprised."

"Surprised? That would be a trick with Porivinar."

"But it could be done." Jared looked thoughtful for a moment. "I can think of at least one thing that would work." After another pause he said, "Keep listening, Yaran. I have some things to check out."

As he left, Jared was thinking about Porivinar's movements before his death. He couldn't figure out why Porivinar would be carried behind the temple if that was not where he was killed. He thought back through the process that had led him behind the temple. A stable boy had told him he saw the captain headed that way, so there were a limited number of places he could have been killed. From the caravansary west and north there was nothing, not even farms.

He had immediately gone around the temple, but he had never thought to look inside. It was universally assumed that you didn't go into old Enzar temples unless you had a specific reason to do so and a particular plan in mind. Despite the many stories of people getting killed in such places, it really wasn't all that likely that a temple that had been sitting by the main road for 3,000 years was going to have active traps in it. It was just that the phrase "old Enzar temple" had come to be synonymous with "you're going to die."

So would Porivinar have checked inside? Jared was certain that he would have done so, and that he must have done so. Without thinking to go get some help, he set out for the temple.

There were few gaps in the wall, but one could enter from the east side in a couple of places. He kept low as he approached and carefully peeked around the corner. Inside he was shocked to see the light of a number of torches and numerous armed figures. It looked like a small army was camped inside.

So this was why the captain had died! He had obviously heard or seen something that made him suspect that there were enemies hiding there, and he had gone to check. Unfortunately, he'd done it in daylight and someone had been waiting for him. He didn't stop to ask why someone who had a body quite well concealed in a building nobody wanted to enter would take it outside and leave it lying around to be found.

He heard something fly past his head, and suddenly he remembered how completely vulnerable he was. Not only could he be surprised in the darkness, he could be overwhelmed by numbers. He would die so quickly nobody at the caravansary would be likely to notice. He started to run and didn't stop until he was almost inside the caravansary compound. Then he stopped and tried to compose himself so that he wouldn't be so noticeable as he crossed it. He retrieved his horse and rode quickly back to the hidden encampment.

A company of Aagerinar elite scouts was a fluid organization, usually consisting of one or two platoons of 20 or so persons each and several teams that could be any size smaller than a platoon. Jared's company had two platoons, his own and Qerelir's, and five 5-man security teams.

He gathered Qerelir and the team leaders quickly and didn't ask for discussion—he just gave out orders. Three teams were sent to add security to Jerald's meeting, two to warn and help protect the Ecumenical Temple. If needed, they were to support the baronial heir's security. The temple was important, being headed by a priestess loyal to the Duke, but it was not as critical as having a baron here who would truly acknowledge his duties to his lord.

Qerelir had questions, but she came from a long tradition of Kelaru scouts, and they knew how to take orders. They were full of advice when asked, but when ordered, they obeyed. Jared might have feared she would regard herself as his superior. In fact, his few days of seniority meant everything to her. She wished she was senior, but she wasn't, and that settled it as far as she was concerned.

Jared elected to stay with the teams in town. Qerelir was an excellent tactician. If she couldn't win the battle around the temple, he knew he probably wouldn't make any difference.

Qerelir put one platoon in a loose line designed to cover as much ground as possible and kept the second ready to respond quickly wherever an attack might come. Jared had ordered her not to try to attack the force in the temple. The scouts had the superior firepower in the open. Inside the building they could be easily trapped and destroyed. She was happy to obey those orders. But there was something that bothered her about this situation, and after a few minutes of waiting she started to mentally list her concerns.

1. Why hide troops in the temple? Besides superstition, which would make it hard to get most troops to stay inside, there were caravan guards all over the town and caravansary. Nobody worried about another few armed men running around Jevlir.
2. How would they get to town without being spotted and stopped? Jared wanted her to meet them before they got to the caravansary so as to keep from involving the civilians there, but there was no way to get to town except over the bridge, and one person could notice them there and report them. Qerelir agreed that they did not want the fight to be at the caravansary itself.
3. Why had they made it so obvious? It was almost as though they wanted someone to find the captain's body.

With that thought she became certain. She could not abandon the watch here just because she was certain that she was guarding the town against nothing. She called her sergeant over and told him to take command. Then she slipped forward into the night and approached the temple herself. It was the work of a few minutes to get a look through the same break in the wall that Jared had used. Inside she saw the torches, but with more time to check she looked carefully at what was casting the shadows. She couldn't get a very clear look. She took out a magical lens, a gift from her father, also a scout. It allowed her to look for the magical lines of force.

And there it was—the magical manipulation of the light, producing shadows on the walls and the appearance of torches set around the walls. Jared had no such device, and had had little time to look, but she was now certain.

She backed away from the wall and immediately whistled a command to her troops. They mounted quickly, and her sergeant brought her horse to her. Then they galloped for Jevlir. Qerelir hoped she wasn't too late.

In the meantime Jared was thinking very similar thoughts. He could feel an attack coming. The hair on the back of his neck was standing up. It was not outside near the temple, but here in town that the attack would come. His security teams were inside the building could take care of anyone there. He was watching the street.

The team leader of the one team he'd kept outside approached him and asked him if he had noticed several armed men heading toward the Ecumenical Temple. He had. But he had to keep the teams here. The two teams at the temple would have to take care of themselves.

He wondered if he should send a messenger and call Qerelir back, but it seemed likely that if she hadn't figured things out by the time a messenger got there, she'd be too late, so he kept all his men with him.

At the Ecumenical Temple dozens of followers had come to join in the defense of the temple. The gate was barred, and people were being admitted only on personal recognition. Alina, known as "the pretty priestess," knew very well that a determined attack by as few as a couple dozen people could overrun her temple. She only had three truly trained guards along with her own magic. Her followers were brave and determined, but they had received less than two weeks of training in their spare time.

She and the security teams were quite certain they could see people moving into position, but they could not do anything until there was an attack. It was important to the temple and to the Duke's forces as well that they be seen as totally obedient to the law.

It started with bottles of heating oil and flaming arrows. The temple building was quickly on fire, and there were patches of burning oil around the compound. The security teams were able to take an occasional shot, but it was hard to tell what was happening. It would not be long before they would have to abandon the compound. Clearly that was their attackers' intent.

Alina wondered why they were making the attack so obvious when they could have won quietly without attracting attention. But however much she might question their approach, it was definitely working. Then she heard a cavalry horn giving a signal she didn't recognize and she saw horsemen coming up all the approach streets from every direction.

The fight was remarkably quick, but the the cavalry didn't stop to help them fight the fire. That turned out to be something at which her local followers excelled.

As Qerelir and her troops arrived at the Ecumenical Temple the attack started at the dinner where Jerald, baronial heir, was the guest of honor. The outside security team spotted people approaching from the outside. The main attack, however, came from the audience. Every young officer in the city militia and the baronial guard was there with their weapons.

It was a quick draw of a sword, but one of the security team was watching closely and threw a dagger directly into the man's sword arm. The delay and confusion allowed Jerald himself to draw his sword and step back from the table. Soon everyone was armed and had displayed their chosen sides. The attackers waited for the help that they thought would come from outside. This was to be a massacre, not just an assassination. The security teams didn't want to kill the attackers. They wanted to question them and find out who had hired them.

Minutes went by with everyone looking for someone else to make a false move. It almost looked like the room was frozen in time. Then Jared stepped into the door and addressed the room.

"I don't know if you're aware of it," he said, "But under Aagerinar law if you can prove that you were hired by someone for a job, such as the assassination of a nobleman, then you are not held guilty. The penalty for attempting such an assassination is death, and I have control of the area outside of this building. I'm wondering who would like to be hung tomorrow morning, and who would like to prove to me that you were hired for the job."

There was a clatter of swords on the ground. "How do we prove we were hired?" asked one man.

"Well, you could have a certified hiring document." Jared noticed their blank looks. "Or if you don't have one of those, you could just identify the person who hired you."

They couldn't wait to give him names.

It was a sunny day two weeks later when Jared and Qerelir were both present as the flag of Aagerinar was raised over city hall in Jevlir. Also present was General Ezbah of the Aagerinar Elite Scouts. Several officers had come with her, and both Qerelir and Jared were wondering just who their new commanding officer would be.

In her own informal way Ezbah walked over to the two of them after the ceremony and tossed them new insignia of rank. Both were now captains—equal in rank.

"You're probably wondering what your assignments are," Ezbah said.

"You could say that," said Qerelir smiling.

"We're forming a new company to work the border here. Jared, you get the current one. Qerelir the new one. You'll be working the northern side of the river," she said, looking at Qerelir.

Then she looked at Jared. "You're thinking I either didn't read or ignored your report. You're thinking you don't deserve promotion, and your sense of fairness doesn't let you feel happy about it if you don't deserve it. Well, let me tell you something. I like officers who can learn. I like officers who can evaluate a situation, including their own weaknesses. I couldn't have evaluated your actions any more cogently, nor could I have recommended any better corrective action."

She started to leave, then looked over her shoulder. "Just make damn sure to take the corrective action you recommended!"

AFTER THE FIRE, WHAT?

The first time that Yagac approached the shrine he was carrying a stick he had cut from a tree and sharpened.

"What do you bring for the god?" said the aged priest. Villagers said he had been at the shrine more than a hundred years. His sparse white hair, parchment-like skin stretched over a frail frame, and piercing grey eyes validated the story.

"I bring this spear," said Yagac, his young voice trembling.

The priest saw a scrawny boy who might have been in his teens, though he could be taken for younger. He knew the villagers had very little to eat.

"That? That's a stick."

"It's a spear. My father says that the God accepts whatever is the best you can bring. You must let me offer it."

The priest thought a moment. It was true that he had told the villagers the god would accept their best. He had meant "only their best" but perhaps this **was** the best the boy could offer. It wouldn't do to give the villagers the idea of withholding things.

"Go in, offer it, and say your prayers."

Inside, Yagac laid his spear on the altar, then prayed. "You know that the lord in the castle takes what he wants. Now he has even taken my sister. I would like you to do something about it."

He felt very peaceful and wanted to laugh–a joyful laugh. But he didn't do either. He put on a sober look and walked from the shrine.

"Did you receive peace?" asked the priest.

"I wasn't praying for peace," said Yagac. Then he walked off toward the village.

The second time Yagac came to the shrine he was carrying a knife made of flint. It was very well formed, and had a wooden handle attached to it with some twine that looked hand woven.

This time the priest just waved him in. At the same time he got an idea. Why not benefit from the boy's repeated returns?

Inside, Yagac laid his knife on the altar, then prayed. "You know that the lord in the castle takes what he wants. Now he has even taken my sister. I would like you to do something about it."

This time the peace and joy that came over him was nearly overwhelming. He was sure there was some divine presence in the shrine. But he wasn't satisfied. He carefully straightened his face as he walked out past the priest.

The priest stopped him. "If you come again to offer a weapon, you must bring food with it. The guards from the castle will be suspicious if they see you bringing weapons as sacrifices. Traditionally they are sacrifices to give one courage and victory in battle."

Yagac nodded and walked away toward the village.

The third time Yagac came to the shrine he was carrying a basket with some vegetables in it. Amongst the vegetables was a very respectable hammer made of a hard rock carefully attached to a wooden handle.

This time the priest decided to make use of provisions he had made to listen to the prayers of worshipers. He had ignored the boy because he figured he was praying for some childish thing and he had no interest.

Inside, Yagac laid his basket on the altar, pulled the hammer out and put it beside the basket, then prayed. "You know that the lord in the castle takes what he wants. Now he has even taken my sister. I would like you to do something about it."

This time the feeling of peace and joy truly was overwhelming. Yagac fell on the floor laughing hysterically. Then he got up, straightened the rags he wore for clothes, wiped any smile from his face, and left.

The priest intercepted him. "You have been touched by the god. I can see it on you. You should be satisfied with what has happened. His peace and joy have come upon you."

"I wasn't praying for peace and joy," said Yagac.

A bit of fear came over the priest. He liked the way things were in the village and at the shrine. While the village produced little, something came to him from everyone, and then he received a monthly payment from the castle lord for help in keeping the villagers quiet.

It wasn't that he didn't believe in the god, though he had never seen anything that could definitely be credited to his activity. The peace and joy? That was a secret ingredient in the incense.

"Be very careful what you pray for, child," he said, trying for a fatherly expression and tone. "The gods always demand much of those they aid! Be happy with his peace, lest you find the price of an answer too high."

He didn't say this because he thought anything might happen. He just didn't want word of a child with such a prayer getting back to the village. He considered reporting the child to the castle guards, but he decided there was no real threat. He'd just bring trouble on himself.

The final time Yagac went to the shrine he was running. He was carrying a short sword in its scabbard. He could barely carry it and run. The priest could hear the sound of horses' hoofs further in the distance. He moved to block the boy, but he was old and slow, and the boy ran directly into the shrine.

Yagac slammed the sword down on the altar and said, "You know that the lord in the castle takes what he wants. Now he has even taken my sister. I would like you to do something about it."

But this time he continued. "I don't want peace. I don't want joy. I want *revenge*. I want things *changed*. I don't care what it costs."

The guards were already outside the door, and the priest turned away so as not to see the boy killed. The priest didn't really believe anything else might happen.

Suddenly the ground shook. Something emerged from the temple, but it wasn't anything that could be recognized as Yagac. As it took steps the ground shook. Fire surrounded it. The guards fled in terror.

Yagac felt no different. He was still just Yagac, just a boy. But as he returned from the castle, riding into the village on a horse he had appropriated, the villagers bowed down in the street, hailing him as a conquering hero.

He was no hero! He was Yagac, who could plow the straightest furrow. Yagac, who loved his family and missed his sister. He'd found her dead in the castle. It wasn't fair! These people wanted food. They wanted protection.

Yagac spurred his horse and rode down the trail away from the village. But even as he did it he knew he would be returning. The god demanded it.

He was also Yagac the responsible, and he would pay the price.

[3]Our God comes
but he doesn't keep silent.
Fire devours before him,
A furious windstorm surrounds him.
— Psalm 50:3

THE CALL

Once in a lifetime, perhaps, a king's knight would ride over the hill to the south of the village. His armor would be gleaming, his clothing immaculate, and his weapons beyond the comprehension of the villagers.

He would come to the center of the village, order that all the young people be assembled, and then he would look from one to another. If he saw one he liked for the king's service, he would call that one. He would say that the one called could refuse, but few believed that. Even fewer believed that the one called would ever be seen again, though they couldn't agree on precisely how long ago anything like this had actually happened.

Even more rarely, never in living memory of the villagers, a king's knight would appear, it was said, to settle quarrels between neighboring lords, to deal with bandits, or to administer the law.

They assumed that the one called would be trained to fight the king's battles, and none of them particularly cared for that. It was hard enough fighting for their local lord, who required his tenants to carry spears and march to battle with neighboring lords if there was a dispute. These disputes were always short, because it was said that if they got too wild or too long, the king would intervene.

But nobody could remember that ever happening, and there were many who believed it was all a lie, a story told and retold to keep people in line.

But one fine spring day while planting was in full swing and nobody was happy for the interruption, over the hill came just such a knight. His armored gleamed like a mirror, and he had with him three riding horses, though he wore his full armor and rode his war horse as he entered the village.

He found the headman and told him to assemble the young people of the town from age 15 to 25, both boys and girls here in the center of the village. The headman didn't want to do this, and the farmers didn't want their children brought in from the fields. They certainly didn't want one of them to ride away on one of those empty horses.

But tradition was strong, and fear even stronger, so the young people were assembled. The knight passed from one to the next, looking and then passing on. He stopped in front of Hedder, a young lady of 17. Hedder had fine, golden hair but otherwise she looked too heavy duty to be considered pretty. Handsome, yes. Pretty, no.

She also asked too many questions and frightened her parents and the headman who liked their world orderly and secure. She was a good babysitter, and a fine farm worker. In fact, other than all those questions, few could find fault with her, though it was said that many young men of the village had begged their parents not to arrange a marriage with her, which explained why she was not betrothed.

"Come, follow me," said the knight to Hedder.

"No!" cried the headman, thinking of what this apparent honor might suggest to the other girls of the village. He had never imagined that the order to include the girls meant that one actually might be called in this way.

"No!" cried Hedder's father, thinking about all the planting to be done and how fast his large and heavy duty daughter was at this work.

"No!" cried her mother, half for her daughter, and half for the girl who took care of all the children, allowing her to accomplish her household work.

But Hedder simply let the hoe she had carried fall and stepped toward the knight. Before most of he villagers had time to recover from surprise, she was seated on one of those horses, riding out of the village.

Many years passed, and the call of Hedder became legend among the villagers. There were those who had been young when it happened who openly questioned whether such a thing had ever occurred. Those who had been there assured them it had, but they didn't believe.

"It's much like the intervention of the king," they would say. "Everybody talks about it, but it never happens. Nobody can even remember it happening."

"The king will intervene if it's necessary, we know he will," said the elders. But deep inside they doubted as well.

"There is no king," said the younger folk, "and even if there is, he just calls our young people. He doesn't intervene."

It happened that very month that the local lord felt that his neighbor had overstepped his bounds, and had moved boundary markers, giving himself more land. Words were exchanged, and finally blows. Then both men went back and summoned their tenants to get out their spears and come to war.

The two armies moved boundary markers back and forth, and occasionally killed one another with spears. The men needed to go to the harvest, but the lords would not allow them to leave.

"Not until all the boundary markers are restored!" said the one.

"Not until my enemy is hanging from a tree for all the damage he's caused!" said the other.

Nobody knew that one of the village headmen had sent a messenger to find one of the king's knights before all the harvest was ruined in the field. He didn't tell anyone, because people would think him foolish. If the messenger returned with help, he would be vindicated. If not, he thought, perhaps the messenger would never return.

Finally one day the two sides gathered across a field from one another. It looked like finally there would be a big battle and one side or the other would win decisively. As they got in formation, lowered their spears and prepared to charge at one another, there was a commotion to the south.

It was a knight, with armor polished and shining, but with a sword out in his hand. Slowly the knight rode between the battle lines. The men looked at their spears and thought that there was really no use trying them against that armor.

As the knight reached the center, both lords came out to meet him.

"I have a right to defend my land!" said the one.

"I have a right to defend myself against this maniac!" said the other.

The knight removed his helmet. Golden hair flowed out. In a feminine voice, soft but firm and authoritative Hedder said: "I would suggest you reconsider. I am called by the king, and he likes his servants to live in peace."

"Follow me!" — Mark 1:17 (and many others)

A State of Mind

The certain mind sees things as it will use them.
– Ancient Enzar Proverb

On a high hill overlooking the harbor bay stood an ancient tower. The lower part of it was covered with grass and vines, but the upper part still stood clean and looked unworn and unweathered, as though standing there for millenia had meant nothing to it.

To the north and a bit east there was the town, nestled amongst hills and the ruins of a much larger city. The villagers called it Ukaz. Most of the time it was a peaceful town.

This particular morning a girl stood on the path just where the steps that led up to the base of the tower ended. I call her a girl, but she was actually in her late 20s. Yet she looked young and perhaps vulnerable. She would be thought beautiful. She was wearing a simple dress that fell below her knees. It was relatively shapeless. She also wore sandals, and her hair was tied in a knot at the back of her head.

"Laaraalindarinaaz," she said to herself. There was nobody else to hear, which was a good thing. She had been told her name was Laranaz, but her parents called her Lara, and the villagers generally called her La.

"Laaraalindarinaaz," she said again, carefully lengthening the pronunciation of each of the double vowels. She was certain from her research that this was her real name, the one from which Laranaz has been derived, or rather had developed due to laziness and unwillingness to maintain the traditions.

Her parents said that names had been shortened just enough to remind everyone that they had a special calling and special abilities in order to carry it out. Her parents said many things. Her parents thought many things. Most of the things her parents said were wrong. She was convinced of that.

Yet she hesitated at the stairs. She was supposed to go on and warn the folks in the fields to bring in whatever food they could find. Sails had been spotted approaching the bay, and within the next two hours the pirates would arrive on the dock, demanding what they wanted of the villagers.

Lara—Laaraalindarinaaz, she corrected herself mentally—had two duties. First to inform the farmers that food was required, then to go with her parents to the dock to meet the pirates. Ever since she had begun to grow up "that way" as her mother said, she was one of those the pirates "enjoyed." Yet despite everything, her father had refused to think of arming to meet the pirates. There were not many of them, and they weren't that strong. The village could have resisted.

"No," her father would say in his quiet voice, "that is not our way. We are people of peace."

"Yet once we were people of war," she had said.

"Do not even think of that!" he exclaimed. "We have paid for those days. We now live for peace, our peace, and the peace of the villagers around us. We have great power, and with that great power comes great responsibility."

Lara didn't see much in the way of power. In fact, she didn't see any. Her people were stronger, faster, and seemed more intelligent than their neighbors, but power? No, she didn't see any of that.

So here she stood looking at the stairs and wondering if she could make herself turn and climb.

"The Enzaru way is simple." She repeated the words of one of the forbidden books to herself. "Ego, knowledge, certainty, ruthlessness, implacability. Ego is the knowledge that the self is one's sole concern. Knowledge is possession of correct, verified information. Certainty is the complete trust in one's judgment needed to act on one's knowledge. Ruthlessness does not regard the consequences to others as one proceeds. Implacability means that nothing and nobody is permitted to stand in the way."

I have the knowledge, she thought. I have verified it and I know it's correct. I'm certain I can carry out my intention and that nobody will stand in my way. It must be the ego that's lacking. I'm asking myself if I have the right to make this decision for our entire village.

She looked again at the inscription. Large portions were missing, not from erosion but from some inconceivable explosion. Her father said it was some sort of rhyming jingle from the ancients, but she couldn't see where rhyming was an activity of the ancients. What was here was simple certainty, certainty that had stretched itself to apparent arrogance.

The inscription told her simply that there were two types of protection for the tower. Magic didn't often fade, and she would assume that it was there in full force. The first level of protection was a series of tricks and traps that would be known to people authorized to enter the tower, or that could be figured out by someone of reasonable competence. If she had read the inscription correctly—no, she paused to correct herself—she had read it correctly, and it meant that there were four layers. The ancients divided this type of security into categories, each double that of the previous. A single layer of security was considered a joke, then there would be two, four, eight, and rarely sixteen. On very rare occasion there might be thirty-two, but that was carrying things a bit far. She would have to figure her way through four layers.

It was the other security that bothered her more, and if she had calculated correctly she could not afford that uncertainty. Uncertainty was making her uncertain. She shook herself. She couldn't go on this way. She was right. Her knowledge was certain, verified (at least insofar as one could do so without actually traversing the steps), and absolute.

She was of the leaders of the town. She was descended from the rulers of the ancient city. That would only carry her so far with ancient magical and intelligent defenses. What she had realized just the day before was that the key elements of proving leadership amongst Enzaru were that boldness and ruthlessness. She could start with a reasonable claim, but she must move on to realizing that she, of all the Enzaru in the town, was the only one who would or could traverse these steps. She was the rightful ruler because she truly did have the might!

With that she took her first step up the stairway. She felt slightly surprised when nothing at all happened. *I can't afford to think this way. There is no reason that anything should happen. I must be certain. No, I **am** certain.*

Another step and then another, and her confidence grew. There was, in fact, no resistance. She was simply climbing some stairs. She even started to worry about her father's reaction, something she hadn't considered. The only end to this mission, she had concluded, would be death or control of the magical powers of the tower, and an end to the pirates.

She nearly set her foot down on the next step before she realized she had reached the first stage of the four stage trap, and it didn't occur on the first of the four platforms. *Tricky!*

There was a skeleton lying face down on the platform ahead of her. It had fallen forward from the very step she had been about to stand on. A brief inspection showed her the bar that would swing out to hit her should she put her foot on that one step. She was about to step past it directly onto the platform when she thought better of it. A bit more examination showed her that there was a pattern in the rock of the platform. A path appeared to her in that pattern as she watched.

She looked at the body as she passed. She couldn't tell much about it, though there was surviving equipment that she would have loved to examine. All that would have to wait. Three more flights of stairs and three more platforms. And somewhere along the way she must encounter the *real* security.

At the second platform she encountered traps that partook of what the ancients would have called "minimal" magic. What that meant was that the traps did not actually use magic for their effect, but they might be assisted by magic. A little telekinesis reloaded crossbows and such simple things.

This still meant that everything required a physical trigger, one that she could spot. And indeed she found that spotting these triggers was simple. When she had disarmed four traps she stopped for a moment to think. It was the first time she had considered the difference between the philosophy of the ancients and that of her own parents.

These traps were clearly not intended to prevent an actual security threat to the tower, but rather to catch trespassers. Some things she had read began to make sense. The attitude toward people reflected in these traps frightened her, now that she was actually seeing it. A trespasser who was unable to find the traps would die.

She continued up the stairs between the second and third platform As she climbed she felt tired. She wondered if the stairs had been longer than she had thought. Then she began to wonder if she really wanted to be here. The ancients were just too ruthless and cruel. She wanted to be a bit more violent than her parents, but not this violent. Just violent enough to get rid of the pirates.

She almost turned around to start down the stairs before she realized what was happening. She looked around to try to find the source, but then realized she didn't need to know the source. This was her first test of authority. Was she one of the natural rulers, or one of the ruled?

"Sufficient force," she said to herself, "means enough force to be ruler rather than ruled. Then she started to take the steps toward the next platform firmly and quickly. "I have a right to be here," she thought, "and I will not be turned back."

She had thought the pressure in her head would fade, but instead it suddenly disappeared, and she was simply climbing some stairs on a sunny morning.

And a fine morning it was. She was on top of the world, completely in control There would obviously be no difficulty at all dealing with the traps that were ahead. Her foot was in the air and descending on a fairly obvious pressure plate before she realized what was happening. It took all of her skill and agility to take a step back and avoid the trap.

That was a fairly obvious test and she nearly failed it. Mental pressure and control could take the form of euphoria as well as depression.

It was again a matter of minutes to discover the path through the third platform, though this time she was certain that a number of the villagers would have been unable to navigate the path even if they had been instructed about the traps and told precisely where to step.

One step up the stairs toward the final platform changed everything in the moment. Thus far she had found and avoided every danger, but when her foot touched that first step she realized immediately that she had erred. She was jumping backward even as she heard something snap to her left, and felt a pain in her left ankle. But she had more to worry about than that, as her right foot had landed on a paving stone that simply fell through. She knew about it, but in jumping back had not had time to avoid it.

Her only hope, she knew, was to push off with her left foot, and then land on just the right stones. And she did land on just the right place, but did so hard and off balance, and felt a pain shoot up her right leg. She wasn't sure if she had broken her right ankle or just sprained it, but she had to place her weight on it in any case. The pain suggested that something was broken, but she stepped forward nonetheless.

Each step was now agony, and she had to check each and every step as she moved forward. The tower loomed immediately above her and seemed threatening.

Between pain, anger, and frustration that she had missed an obvious trap she felt determination come through.

I am certain.

I am ruthless.

I am implacable.

I will use this tower to defend my family and my village from the pirates.

Immediately she felt a new assault on her mind and her senses. She saw an army on the coming through the valley to the south, marching toward the tower. A beam of light, varying in color, came from the tower and played over the ranks of the approaching army. First they charged forward, then they broke and began to run, but the beam of light sought them out. Finally there was only one person trying to escape over the crest of a hill, and the light followed him, seemingly carelessly, but finally killing him just before he would have passed to safety.

It seemed that she was being asked if she approved of this action. Her first thought was that it was a test. The intelligence of the tower would only allow the most ruthless and implacable of people to enter. But then she thought again: *It's not up to the tower to decide and ask me to approve. I am the ruler. It is up to the tower to be my tool.*

She stepped forward, thinking a command: Prepare for action.

For several moments the pressure continued on her mind, and various visions fought for her attention. She ignored them, repeating only the thought, "Prepare for action."

She arrived at the tower. She had gotten the idea that the place was somehow automated. According to what she had read the ancients were quite capable of doing so, trapping some soul or spirit inside and requiring it to control the devices. But when she arrived, she found that she had to open the door herself. Though she found no traps or other security devices she also found nothing that might be used to control any weaponry.

She knew she was running out of time, and she was still a long way from the top of the tower from which that beam had come. Somehow, she had not been noticing the pain in her ankles for the last few minutes.

She found herself running up the stairs, giving only a cursory glance for further traps. She didn't believe the garrison would have had traps set around the tower itself. She wasn't certain why, but she had expected that a tower that so clearly had survived the last battle around her home town would have been filled with weapons and bodies, but the place was relatively clean.

What was even more surprising was the room at the top of the tower that controlled the weapon she had seen in vision. It was entirely mechanical. She had gotten the idea that the ancients used magic even when simpler methods would have worked, but this thing was designed to be operated by several people. She was able to recognize when magic was in use, and the only magic here was in the center of the weapon itself, which was much like a round mirror that could be pointed in any direction.

It was designed for control by more than one person, preferably four, but she only needed to aim it once. She arranged the mirror to point at the pirate ship. This was easier than she had planned. She had hoped to get magical weapons which she could then wield in an attack on the pirates herself.

With the weapon aimed and her hand on the trigger she heard her father say, "The ancients always turned to violence. Once you turn to violence, you have no other choice. Violence will always lead to more violence."

"Well," said Laaraalindarinaaz, "I make the choice of my ancestors." With that she pressed the trigger. As legend said, most weapons of the ancients that remained physically intact also still carried their full magic, and this was no exception. The ship disappeared. A huge cloud of steam rose from the harbor. Part of the wharf disappeared as well.

There might have been some of her own people there as well, but there wouldn't be any pirates left. They had not quite reached their place at the pier.

It was hours later before she returned to the town. She had found the armory and equipped herself quite handsomely. She even knew how to use some of the weapons she had. Rumor had it that it only took one discovery of ancient Enzar weapons and armor to make an individual's career.

She entered the town. Her father came to meet her. "Please, my daughter," he said. "You have gotten rid of the pirates. Do not return to the ways of the ancients."

But there was also the chief of the farmers to the south. They had seen the weapon in action, and so had the others, he thought, to the south. "You will have to get ready to defend the tower. Others will know someone has been there and will want its treasure."

"Yes," she replied. "I will stay in the tower tonight. Tomorrow we prepare for war."

Only a true Enzar can truly use Enzar weapons.

– Ancient Enzar Saying

JUSTICE SEEKER

Her knock was soft, fearful, diffident. Aymaran could not have said precisely why he attached all those adjectives to a simple knock, but he did.

"Enter," he said, choosing the local Malkuthim dialect.

For a moment, he thought the person at the door hadn't heard him, but just as he was about to yell again, she pushed the door open. Aymaran saw a small woman, around a meter and a half in height, dressed in a long colorful skirt and a blouse with the collar buttoned tightly around her neck. She looked frightened and desperate.

She handed him a card and asked, "Are you Aymaran? Seeker of justice?"

He looked at the card. It was one of his. It read simply:

Aymaran
Seeker of Justice
#2 New Temple Row

It was otherwise unadorned. He had spread them around the city quite indiscriminately.

He studied the expression on her face. She looked like a woman who had been tried beyond the limits of her endurance, but did not give up, because she was the kind of person who simply *refused* to give up.

"Tell me your story," he said, leaning back in his chair to listen.

She looked at him for a moment. He looked relaxed and unconcerned. In fact, he looked much more like a professor than any sort of detective or attorney. He just continued to look at her and wait.

"I'm from the kingdom of Kallasia," she began. "My husband and I along with our three children are, uh, were traveling to Aroqra down the coast and our ship put in here in Aagerinar to exchange some cargo.

"We chose to stay at the Inn of the Night on the Town. I remember that my husband..."

She choked up and paused briefly, then resumed. "My husband commented that the name was strange, but the inn has a reputation in all the ports of the Western Sea. That is, Eastern Sea as you call it here."

"During the evening's dance my husband was bringing me a drink and someone bumped into him. One thing led to another and he tripped a couple who fell sprawling on the floor. Apologies were offered all around and the waiters cleaned up the mess, but I could see that one man was very angry even though he was doing his best to control it in front of the crowd.

"I thought the evening had returned to normal, but about an hour later I noticed that my oldest son was missing. He'd been at the table next to us along with his two younger sisters.

"The girls told us that he had gone outside. My husband rushed out to look for him. Even though he's sixteen, he knows nothing about city life, and certainly nothing about this city.

"My husband didn't come back in, and I was about to go outside myself to check, when my son came running back in the door and yelled, 'He shot him!'

"Shot who?" I asked.

"Dad," he said.

"Well, I rushed out and there in the alley next to the inn was my husband flat on the ground. At the other end of the alley was the man who had been so angry during the dancing. He was holding a small crossbow. He just stood there watching.

"The police came, and he claimed my husband had attacked him and he had shot him in self defense. There were some witnesses—I don't know how many—who agreed with him. My son just kept saying, "I killed him." The police never got any sense from him, and neither have I.

"I didn't know what to do. The Temple of the Light buried my husband the next day, which took a good deal of money even though the temple took me on as a charity case.

"That was the day before yesterday. We had to move to a cheaper inn. Again, my son went missing. I couldn't find him anywhere. Then this morning, I was called to the city guard headquarters and told that he had attempted to kill some very important merchant, name of Argaz. It turns out Argaz is the same as the man who killed my father.

"I tried to get an attorney, but even after paying a consultation fee, the attorneys tell me there is really no chance. They say it would be much better if he *had* killed Argaz, though I don't understand it. They called it the 'he had it coming' defense.

"Now I'm told that Jarel, that's my son, will go on trial tomorrow and if the attorneys are to be believed he'll be convicted and could be executed."

She paused for a long time and Aymaran simply let her gather her thoughts. Fighting tears she continued. "I've lost my husband, and now I'm about to lose my son. I have no more resources. I don't even know if it's justice. All I know is I can't take this loss."

"A sergeant in the city guard gave me your card, and you're all I have left."

At the last statement, Aymaran leaned forward. "Would you remember the name of the sergeant?"

"I'm not sure. It started with 'O' I think, Oroda, maybe."

Aymaran made a note. "Now, he said, I need to ask you a few questions."

"I'll do my best," she said.

"When you entered the alley, did you enter from the north or the south end?"

She thought a moment. "I went out the main entrance to the inn and turned left, then left again into the alley."

"South, then," said Aymaran. "And where was your husband?"

"He was further in, lying on his face."

"Good. Now where was Argaz?"

"Standing in the entrance to the alley. I had to go around him to get to my husband."

"And which way was your husband facing?"

"Well, he was lying on his face, with his head toward the entrance to the alley."

"And did you see whether he had been shot in the front or in the back?"

"No, there was blood everywhere."

"Did you see a crossbow bolt or an arrow?"

"No. Just blood. So much blood!"

"And your son, Jarel, hasn't told you anything."

"Nothing, except that his dad was trying to rescue him, which I don't understand. He'd just gone exploring, and my husband was looking for him, not rescuing him, but he wouldn't explain. Now they won't even let me see him."

"Very well," said Aymaran, "I'll take a look at this."

"What should I do?"

"Go back to your inn room and do your best not to be seen. I'll talk to you before the trial and let you know what to do."

Aymaran thought for some time after the lady had left. It was not difficult to figure out what had happened. He would have to ask a few questions, but he was pretty sure he knew what he would find. The problem was how to use that information effectively.

He was stuck with defending the boy, who had walked up to his target with a crossbow and fired in front of doubtless at least dozens of witnesses. The attorneys had advised the woman correctly—from their point of view. It was indeed extremely difficult to manage the "he had it coming" defense when the victim was still alive to speak for himself.

The "he had it coming" defense was a distinctly Enzar twist to a basically Ardenean system of law. The Enzar had rarely tried someone for murder, tending to think that if you let someone kill you, you didn't really deserve to live. But if you did it very openly and without excuse, or you did it to someone to whom you had an obligation, you were likely to be charged and tried.

Modern Aagerinar, however had a basically Ardenean system of law, and the concept had been incorporated in a somewhat different form. The defense involved charging the victim with having done something deserving of whatever had been done to him or her.

In this case, had Jarel actually killed Argaz, he could claim that Argaz had killed his father, that the police had not arrested him, but that Argaz "had it coming." The trial would then not be about whether or not Jarel had actually killed Argaz; it would be about whether Argaz had killed Jarel's father. The prosecution and defense switched places in a sense, and the Ducal prosecutor was then obliged to defend the victim.

Why not just go to the police and give them evidence and have Argaz charged? Simply because the burden of proof did not shift with this defense. Rather than having to prove beyond reasonable doubt that Argaz had killed his father, Jarel would simply have to prove that it was reasonable for him to believe that Argaz had unjustfiably killed his father.

The solution could be risky. He had to be sure of his ground, but he was thought he had a good chance of resolving this situation and doing a service to the city at the same time.

It was late in the evening when Aymaran found Sergeant Orodan, as his name turned out to be. At first the sergeant didn't want to talk to him at all or even to acknowledge that he was the person who had given the lady Aymaran's card.

"I don't think I'll need you to testify," Aymaran assured Sergeant Orodan.

"I won't testify, not against Argaz," he said, inadvertently confirming his identity.

"But you were not happy with the results of the investigation."

"No. I doubt that the foreigner was armed. He had a knife on him, but as far as I could tell it hadn't been taken from his belt, and there were no marks on his belt where the hilt was attached."

"Was the crossbow bolt in his back or his chest?"

"That's another problem. There was no bolt. We couldn't find one. 'It fell into the sewers,' says the Lieutenant, but the hole didn't go through. And yes, it went into his back."

"Odd, that."

"Yes, and what's more, it looked like the body had been moved. I would guess that the man was standing in the entrance to the alley, facing south, and was shot from further down the alley from behind."

"Which would make self defense unlikely."

Orodan laughed bitterly. "Unlikely, yes, but not impossible. You see, one could argue that the drag marks I saw were made by someone else at another time. It's a fairly busy alley, after all. One could argue—and Argaz certainly will—that the man attacked or lunged with the knife and then turned to run when his attack failed. It would be regarded as self defense by the court. So essentially Argaz got away with murder. That's my opinion."

"But you won't testify."

"No. Now don't blame me. I can see that look in your eyes. If I testified to all of that, there would still be some doubt it was murder, especially in the eyes of a jury."

"You could look down in the sewers for the bolt."

"I could, but I don't actually think it's down there, and no matter how hard I look and *don't* find it someone is going to say I missed it."

"But what about the boy?"

"I never saw any boy, not until afterward."

This interview confirmed precisely what Aymaran had concluded. Most likely Irina's husband had been lured outside by the absence of his son. Whether Argaz had taken advantage of the son's natural tendency to wander, or had perhaps even lured Jarel outside as well didn't matter that much.

The next morning Aymaran arrived early at the inn where Irina was staying. He found her awake in her room.

"I have a plan, but you are going to have to trust me—trust me even though things will look bad."

Irina looked at him for a moment. She seemed more composed. "I have no choice. When I said you were my last chance, I really meant it."

"How much money do you have?"

"I have about 2,000 in Kallasian royals, but I was saving most of it to get my daughters and myself back to Kallasia. There's no point in us going on."

"I'm going to need it."

"What for?"

"I think if I explained it, it would make it worse. You're going to have to choose to trust me."

She only hesitated a moment. "What choice do I have?"

Under the mattress in a bag was her money. She handed it over —everything she had.

"I also need you to sign this," said Aymaran, handing her an official looking parchment. "It instructs me to use your money according to your son's instructions," he continued, but before he completed the statement she had signed without more than a glance.

At City Guard headquarters Aymaran was permitted to see the prisoner. Despite his slogan "seeker of justice" he had not imagined he would actually have to use his official membership in the Guild of Advocates, but today it came in handy.

Jarel had obviously given up. "You want to be my advocate?" he asked.

"Yes."

"Why? There's no chance. I'm dead."

"I don't have much time. I need you to sign two documents. The first assigns me as your advocate. The second says that I must use some money I got from your mother for a particular purpose. It would be best if you would sign it without reading it."

"Who cares?" said Jarel, and signed both. If Aymaran had known more about Kallasia he might have been surprised that both the mother and the child could write.

Argaz climbed the steps to he city court of Aagerinar confidently. He assumed that this latest part of his plan to finish off the family of the man who had humiliated him would go without a hitch. As he reached the top step, a knight in shining armor—literally—stepped from behind a column and without hesitation rammed a two-handed sword through him with both hands. There was a flash of light-based magic and more than half of the body disappeared. The knight then withdrew his sword and stood leaning on it. He made no effort to leave.

Argaz's bodyguards were too stunned to react. By the time they decided that they really didn't want to take the knight on face to face, the city guardsmen were already there.

The city guardsmen chose to take the view that a knight who has just rammed a sword through a prominent citizen and then simply stands there likely has some kind of an explanation.

"I am Indros," he said, "Knight of Zakah. I have a contract." He passed a document to the guardsman in question.

At the same time the judge had just sat down at the bench for the trial of Jarel for attempted murder. He was just preparing to select the jury, a rather quick process in Aagerinar, when a guardsman entered and approached the prosecutor.

After a whispered conversation the prosecutor rose. "Your honor, I must request a continuance. It appears that the prisoner has reached out even from his cell and killed his victim. The charges must be investigated and a new case created."

"Challenge," said Aymaran.

"Why?" asked the judge succinctly.

"Because my client is traveling through, and he and his family need to proceed. I am aware of the situation, and am willing to stipulate that my client did, in fact, hire someone to kill Argaz the merchant."

"If you are aware of the situation, then you must be implicated."

"That is indeed true. I transported the document in question from the prisoner to the person contracted to do the killing. I would remind your honor, however, that I cannot be prosecuted unless my client is found guilty."

"Prosecutor?"

"I am assuming my opponent is intending to use the 'he had it coming' defense as it is called colloquially. As such, I need time to investigate the original killing."

"I have no objection to this investigation, but I must point out that since that killing is not in doubt, she will have the task of demonstrating beyond reasonable doubt that the killing was justified. I don't think she can do that."

"That makes no difference at this point," said the judge.

"On the contrary, your honor, I believe it means that my client should be released on bail."

The judge turned to the prosecutor. "Any objection?"

"Your honor, the young man is just passing through our city. What's to guarantee he doesn't simply leave?"

"Well," said the judge, "The argument of council for the defense is very strong. It is vanishingly rare for a 'he had it coming' defense to fail when the target undoubtedly killed a family member of the accused and is now actually dead. Bail is set in the amount of 100 sovereigns."

It was three days later that Irina, Indros, Aymaran, prosecutor Ulanar, and Jarel all met, again at the Inn of the Night on the Town.

"I don't want to sound ungrateful," said Irina, "But I still don't understand how Indros here is not guilty of murder."

"Oh, that's easy," said Ulanar. "Aagerinar law is quite odd. We have an exception based on Enzar law that states that an assassin is not responsible for his actions if he acts solely as the agent of another. While under Enzar law an assassin would not have to name the person who hired him, provided he could convince authorities that he had been hired, under Aagerinar's law he must name the person who hired him, who was then deemed guilty of murder. Only Jarel had a defense."

She turned to Aymaran. "I'm quite glad not to send a 16 year old kid to the gallows for attempting to avenge his father, but I still don't understand how it was accomplished. Nobody seems to have had enough money to truly hire a killing, and a killing which is discounted doesn't count. I had to allow it, because I can't find any standard for hiring a knight of Zakah for a killing."

"Well, it's rather simple," explained Aymaran. "There is no such price, but there could be."

"You see, while everyone knows that the worshipers of Zakah are incredibly legalistic in their own way, and make their own rules about justice, most people also make other assumptions based on that."

"What assumptions?" asked Ulanar.

"The one you made in your investigation. While they generally don't hire themselves out because they might be told to do something they can't approve, they have no rule against getting paid for doing the right thing. They just can't allow the pay to persuade them to do the wrong thing."

"OK, but a contract killing? Don't they take responsibility for their actions with pride?"

"Well, actually they do."

Indros was watching Aymaran with wonder. "You really have studied my religion."

"I am a seeker of justice."

"I see."

"To continue, Ulanar," said Aymaran, "there is also the assumption that they could not take a contract to kill someone. But their religion has a saying that any method that will allow pursuit of justice must be considered. I offered Indros a contract by which he could do something that he would really have liked to do, but I would make it possible for him to do it and survive."

"And," said Ulanar nodding, "by paying someone 2,000 Kallasian royals to do something he actually wanted to do, you made it impossible for me to convince a jury that the price was discounted."

"But how did he convince you he was right?"

"Oh, that was simple. He stepped under the sword of Zakah that hangs over the lintel and swore before my god in my temple that the killing was justified by my standards and that he knew those standards well enough to swear such an oath."

"Good lord," said Ulanar. "That requires some guts! I heard that the sword of Zakah will fall on anyone who swears falsely in his temple."

"Oh well," said Aymaran, "I'm still here!"

The next day Aymaran saw Irina and her family off at the dock. For some reason, even though they had many offers of places to work, they didn't want to stay in the city.

But that was OK. Justice had been done.

Coming Soon from *Energion Publications* fiction …

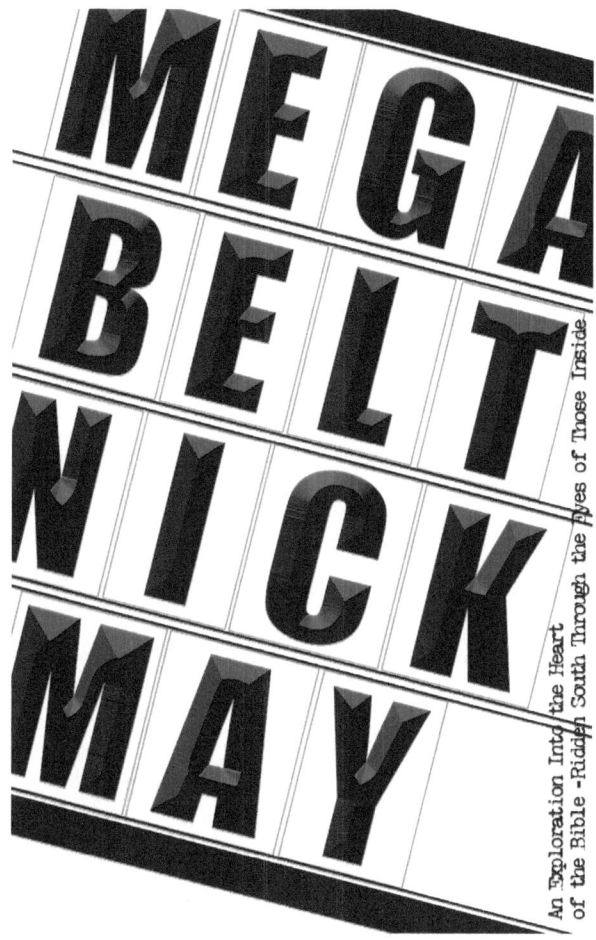

Megabelt is a fictional account of the South and its preoccupations with modern Christianity told from the point of view of a boy named Gil growing up in what is otherwise known as the "Bible Belt."

Join Gil on his journey! Coming October 30, 2009.

Energion Publications, P. O. Box 841, Gonzalez, FL 32560

(850) 525-3916 / energionpubs.com / pubs@energion.com

Also by Henry Neufeld from Energion Publications:

When People Speak for God	$17.99
Not Ashamed of the Gospel	$12.99
What's In A Version?	$12.99
I Want to Pray	$7.99
Disciples: Jesus With Us	$7.99
To the Hebrews: A Participatory Study Guide	$9.99
Revelation: A Participatory Study Guide	$9.99
Identifying Your Gifts and Service:	$9.99
Small Group Edition	$12.99

Generous Quantity Discounts Available

Dealer Inquiries Welcome

Energion Publications
P.O. Box 841
Gonzalez, FL 32560
Website: http://energionpubs.com
Email: pubs@energion.com
Phone: (850) 525-3916

www.ingramcontent.com/pod-product-compliance
Lightning Source LLC
Chambersburg PA
CBHW020154180626
46810CB00004B/1885